Ivan Turgenev

FIRST LOVE

TRANSLATED FROM THE RUSSIAN BY ISAIAH BERLIN

Penguin Books

Penguin Books Ltd, Harmondsworth, Middlesex, England
Penguin Books, 625 Madison Avenue, New York, New York 10022, U.S.A.
Penguin Books Australia Ltd, Ringwood, Victoria, Australia
Penguin Books Canada Ltd, 41 Steelcase Road West, Markham, Ontario, Canada
Penguin Books (N.Z.) Ltd, 182–190 Wairau Road, Auckland 10, New Zealand

—

This translation first published by Hamish Hamilton 1950
Published in Peacock Books 1977
Copyright © Isaiah Berlin, 1950

—

Made and printed in Great Britain by
C. Nicholls & Company Ltd
Set in Monotype Garamond

Translator's Note

My thanks are due to Lady Anglesey for her most valuable assistance at every stage in the preparation of this translation, and to Lord David Cecil and Mr M. W. Dick who kindly consented to read the M.S.

I.B.

THE guests had left long ago. The clock struck half-past twelve. Only the host, Sergey Nicolayevich and Vladimir Petrovich remained in the room.

The host rang the bell and ordered supper to be taken away.

'Well then, that's agreed,' he said, settling himself more deeply into his armchair and lighting a cigar. 'Each of us is to tell the story of his first love. You begin, Sergey Nicolayevich.'

Sergey Nicolayevich, a round little man with a fair, plump face, looked first at his host and then up at the ceiling.

'In my case,' he finally said, 'there was no first love. I began with the second.'

'How do you mean?'

'Oh, it's quite simple. I was eighteen when I first began to court a very charming young girl, but I did this as if it was nothing new to me, exactly as I later flirted with others. Actually I fell in love for the first and last time when I was about six, with my nurse, but that was a very long time ago. I do not now remember the details of our relationship – and even if I did, how could they possibly interest anyone?'

'Well then, what are we to do?' the host began. 'There was nothing very remarkable about my first love either: I didn't fall in love with anyone until I met Anna Ivanovna, my present wife, and then it all went perfectly smoothly. Our fathers arranged the whole thing. We soon grew fond of one another and married shortly after.

7

My tale is soon told. But I must admit, gentlemen, that when I brought up the topic of first love, I was really relying on you old bachelors; not that you are really old – but you're not exactly young, are you? Vladimir Petrovich, won't you regale us with something?'

'My first love was certainly not at all ordinary,' replied Vladimir Petrovich, after a moment's hesitation. He was a man of about forty with dark, slightly greying hair.

'Ah!' said the host and Sergey Nicolayevich with one voice. 'That's much better, tell us the story.'

'Why, certainly ... no; I'd rather not. I'm not good at telling stories. They come out either too bald and dry, or else much too long and quite unreal; but if you'll allow me, I will write down all I can remember and then read it to you.'

At first they would not agree, but Vladimir Petrovich finally had his way. A fortnight later they met again, and Vladimir Petrovich kept his word.

This is what he had written down:

I

I WAS sixteen at the time. It happened in the summer of 1833.

I was living in Moscow, with my parents. They used to take a house for the summer near the Kaluga Toll-gate, opposite the Neskootchny Park – I was preparing for the University, but worked little and slowly.

Nobody interfered with my freedom. I did what I liked, particularly after the departure of my last tutor – a Frenchman who had never got used to the idea that he had been dropped 'like a bomb' (so he said) into Russia; he used to lie in bed helplessly for days on end, with an exasperated expression on his face. My father treated me with good-humoured indifference; my mother scarcely noticed me, although she had no other children; she was absorbed by other cares. My father, who was still young and very handsome, had not married her for love. He was ten years younger than my mother; she led a gloomy life, was in a constant state of irritation and always anxious and jealous – though never in my father's presence. She was very frightened of him – his manner was severely cold and aloof . . . I have never seen anyone more exquisitely calm, more self-assured or more imperious.

I shall never forget the first weeks I spent in the country. The weather was magnificent – we left Moscow on the ninth of May, St Nicholas' Day. I used to go for walks in our garden, or in the Neskootchny Park, or sometimes beyond the Toll-gate; I would take a book with me – Kaidanov's lectures, for example – though I seldom opened it, and spent most of the time repeating lines of poetry aloud to myself – I knew a great many by heart then. My blood was in a ferment within me, my heart was full of longing, sweetly and foolishly; I was all expectancy and wonder; I was tremulous and waiting; my fancy fluttered and circled about the same images like martins round a bell-tower at dawn; I dreamed and was sad and sometimes cried. But through the tears and the melancholy, inspired by the music of the verse or the beauty of the evening, there always rose upwards, like the grasses of early spring, shoots of happy feeling, of young and surging life.

I had a horse of my own; I used to saddle it myself and go riding to some distant place. At times I would break into a gallop, and imagine myself a knight riding in a tournament (how gaily the wind whistled in my ears!) – or, lifting my face up, receive into myself the whole blue radiance of the sky.

I remember that at that time the image of woman, the shadowy vision of feminine love, scarcely ever took definite shape in my mind: but in every thought, in every sensation, there lay hidden a half-conscious, shy, timid awareness of something new, inexpressibly sweet, feminine … This presentiment, this sense of expectancy, penetrated my whole being; I breathed it, it was in every drop of blood that flowed through my veins – soon it was to be fulfilled.

The house we had taken was a wooden building with pillars and had two small, low lodges. In the lodge on the left was a tiny factory for the manufacture of cheap wall-paper. Occasionally I used to wander over to it and watch a dozen or so village boys, lean, tousle-headed, with pinched faces, in long greasy smocks, as they jumped on to wooden levers and forced them down on to the square blocks of the presses, and in this way, by the weight of their shrunken bodies, stamped the brightly coloured patterns on the paper. The other lodge was empty and to let. One day, about three weeks after the ninth of May, the shutters of this lodge were opened and women's faces appeared in the windows – a family had evidently moved in. I remember how that day at dinner my mother asked the butler who our neighbours were, and hearing the name of Princess Zasyekin, first said, not disrespectfully, 'Ah, a princess …', but then she added, 'A poor one, I expect.' 'They came in three cabs, ma'am, and the furniture isn't worth mentioning.' 'Well,' replied my mother, 'it might have been worse.' My father gave her a cold look which silenced her.

And indeed Princess Zasyekin could not have been a rich woman; the house she had taken was so decrepit and narrow and low that no one of even moderate means would have been willing to live there. Actually all this meant nothing to me at the time. The princely title had little effect on me. I had just been reading Schiller's *The Robbers*.

2

I was in the habit of wandering about our garden every evening with a gun looking for crows. I had an inveterate loathing for these wary, cunning and predatory birds. On the day in question I strolled as usual into the garden and, having scoured every walk in vain (the crows knew me and only cawed harshly now and then from afar), I happened to come near the low fence which divided 'our' property from the narrow strip of garden which ran to the right beyond the lodge and belonged to it. I was walking with my head bowed when suddenly I heard the sound of voices. I looked across the fence – and stood transfixed. A strange sight met my gaze.

A few paces from me – on a lawn flanked by green raspberry canes – stood a tall, slender girl in a striped pink dress with a white kerchief on her head. Four young men clustered round her, and she was tapping them one by one on the forehead with those small grey flowers – I do not know their name, but they are well known to children: these flowers form little bags and burst loudly if you strike them against anything hard. The young men offered their foreheads so eagerly, and there was in the girl's movements (I saw her in profile) something so enchanting, imperious and caressing, so mocking and charming, that I nearly cried out with wonder and delight, and should, I suppose, at that moment, have given everything in the world to have those lovely fingers tap my forehead too. My rifle slipped to the grass; I forgot everything; my eyes devoured the graceful figure, the lovely neck, the beautiful arms, the slightly dishevelled fair hair under the white kerchief – and the half-closed, perceptive eye, the lashes, the soft cheek beneath them . . .

'Young man! Hey, young man!' suddenly cried a voice near me. 'Is it proper to stare at unknown young ladies like that?'

I started violently, and almost fainted: near me, on the other side of the fence, stood a man with close-cropped dark hair, looking at me ironically. At the same moment the girl too turned towards me . . . I saw large grey eyes in a bright, lively face, and suddenly this face began to quiver and laugh. There was a gleam of white teeth, a droll lift of the eyebrows . . . I blushed terribly, snatched up my gun, and pursued by resonant but not unkind laughter, fled to my room, threw myself on the bed and covered my face with my hands. My heart leaped within me. I felt very ashamed and unusually gay. I was extraordinarily excited.

After a rest I combed my hair, brushed myself, and came down to tea. The image of the young girl floated before me. My heart was leaping no longer but felt somehow deliciously constricted. 'What is the matter with you,' my father asked suddenly. 'Shot a crow?' I nearly told him everything, but checked the impulse and only smiled to myself. As I was going to bed, without quite knowing why, I spun round two or three times on one foot; then I put pomade on my hair, lay down, and slept like a top all night. Before morning I woke up for an instant, lifted my head, looked round me in ecstasy and fell asleep again.

3

'How can I make their acquaintance?' was my first thought when I woke in the morning. I strolled into the garden before breakfast, but did not go too near the fence and saw no one. After breakfast, I walked several times up and down the street in front of our house – and, from a distance, glanced once or twice at the windows ... I fancied I could see her face behind the curtain; this alarmed me. I hurried away. 'Still, I must get to know her,' I kept thinking, as I paced uncertainly up and down the sandy stretch in front of the Neskootchny Park. 'But how? That is the question.' I recalled the smallest details of yesterday's meeting. For some reason I had a particularly clear image of the way in which she had laughed at me. But as I was frantically making one plan after another, fate was already providing for me.

While I was out, my mother had received from her new neighbour a letter on grey paper, sealed with the sort of brown wax which is only used on Post Office forms, or on the corks of bottles of cheap wine. In this letter, illiterate and badly written, the princess begged my mother for her protection: my mother, the princess wrote, enjoyed the intimate acquaintance of important persons, upon whose favour depended the fortunes of herself and of her children, involved as she was in several vital lawsuits: 'I tern to you,' she wrote, 'az one gentelwoman to another; moreover, I am delited to make use of this oportunity.' Finally, she begged my mother's permission to call upon her. I found my mother in a disagreeable frame of mind: my father was not at home, and she had no one to consult. Not to reply to 'the gentlewoman' – and she was a princess too – was impossible. But how to reply? That worried my mother. To write in French seemed inappropriate – on the other hand, her own Russian spelling was not too certain; she knew this and was not anxious to take the risk. She welcomed my return, therefore, and at once told me to call on the princess and explain to her by word of mouth that she would, of course, at all times be ready to offer any help within her power to her Ladyship, and begged the princess to do her the honour of calling upon her towards two o'clock. This swift and sudden fulfilment of my secret desire at once delighted and alarmed me. I did not, however, show any sign of my inner turmoil; I went first to my room in order to put on my new neck-tie and frock-coat: at home I still went about in a short jacket and turned-down collar – which I simply hated.

4

In the poky and untidy hall of the lodge, which I entered trembling in every limb, I was met by a grey-haired old servant with a face the colour of dark copper, surly little pig's eyes, and the deepest wrinkles on his forehead and temples I had ever seen in my life. He was carrying a plate on which there was a half-picked herring bone; shutting the door which led into the other room with his foot, he snapped: 'What do you want?'

'Is the Princess Zasyekin at home?' I asked.

'Vonifaty!' a cracked female voice screamed from within.

The servant turned without a word, revealing as he did so the threadbare back of his livery with a solitary rusted crested button; he went away, leaving the plate on the floor.

'Have you been to the police station?' said the same female voice. The servant muttered something in reply. 'Eh? Is there somebody there?' said the voice again.

'The young gentleman from next door.'

'Well, show him in.'

'Will you step into the drawing-room, sir,' said the servant, reappearing and picking up the plate from the floor. I collected myself and went into the drawing-room. I found myself in a small and not very tidy room. The furniture was shabby and looked as if no one had bothered to arrange it. By the window, in an armchair with a broken arm, sat a woman of about fifty, plain, her hair uncovered, in an old green dress with a gaudy worsted shawl round her neck; her small, black eyes pierced into me. I went up to her and bowed. 'Have I the honour to address the Princess Zasyekin?'

'I am Princess Zasyekin. And you are the son of Mr V—?'

'That is so, ma'am. I have come to you with a message from my mother.'

'Won't you sit down? Vonifaty, where are my keys? You haven't seen them, have you?'

I conveyed to Mme Zasyekin my mother's reply to her note. She listened to me, drumming upon the window-sill with her fat, red fingers, and when I had finished, once again fixed her eyes upon me.

'Very good. I'll be sure to call,' she remarked at last. 'But how young you are! How old are you, if I might ask?'

'Sixteen,' I replied with a slight falter. The princess extracted from her pocket a bundle of greasy papers covered with writing, lifted them to her nose and began going through them.

'A good age,' she suddenly observed, turning and shifting in her chair. 'Please make yourself at home! We are very simple here.'

'Too simple,' I could not help thinking with disgust, as I took in her unsightly figure.

At that instant, another door flew open and in the doorway there appeared the girl I had seen in the garden the evening before. She lifted her hand, and a mocking smile flitted across her face. 'And here's my daughter,' said the princess, indicating her with her elbow. 'Zinochka, the son of our neighbour, Mr V—. What is your name, if I might ask?'

'Vladimir,' I replied, rising, and stuttering from sheer excitement.

'And your patronym?'

'Petrovich.'

'Yes, I once knew a Chief Constable. He was Vladimir Petrovich too. Vonifaty, don't look for the keys. They are in my pocket.'

The young woman continued to look at me with the same mocking smile, narrowing her eyes a little, and inclining her head slightly.

'I have already seen Monsieur Woldemar,' she began (the silver sound of her voice ran through me with a sort of sweet shiver). 'You will let me call you so?'

'Do, please,' I stammered.

'Where was that?' asked the princess. Her daughter did not answer.

'Are you busy at this moment?' the young woman asked, without taking her eyes off me.

'Oh no, no.'

'Would you like to help me wind my wool? Come with me.' She gave me a little nod and left the drawing-room. I followed her.

In the room we entered, the furniture was a little better and arranged with more taste; though actually, at that moment, I was scarcely able to notice anything. I moved as in a dream, and felt through my entire being an intense, almost imbecile, sense of well-being. The young princess sat down, took a skein of red wool, and pointing to a chair beside her, carefully undid the skein and laid it across my hands. All this she did without a word, with a kind of amused deliberation, and with the same bright, sly smile on her slightly parted lips. She began to wind the wool round a bent card, and then suddenly cast a look at me, a look so swift and radiant that I could not help lowering my eyes for an instant. When her eyes, for the most part half closed, opened to their full extent, her face would be utterly transformed, as if flooded with light. 'What did you think of me yesterday, Monsieur Woldemar?' she asked, after a short pause. 'You disapproved of me, I suppose.'

'I? ... Princess ... I didn't think anything ... How could I?' I replied in confusion.

'Listen,' she said. 'You don't know me yet. I am very strange. I wish to be told the truth always. You are sixteen, I hear, and I am twenty-one. You see, I am much older than you. That is why you must always tell me the truth ... and do what I tell you,' she added. 'Look at me ... Why don't you look at me?'

I was plunged into even deeper confusion; however, I did raise my eyes and look at her. She smiled, not as before, but as if to encourage me. 'Look at me,' she said, lowering her voice caressingly. 'I do not find it disagreeable. I like your face. I have a feeling that we shall be friends. And do you like me?' she added archly.

'Princess,' I was beginning.

'First of all, you must call me Zinaida Alexandrovna, and secondly, how queer that children' (she corrected herself), 'that young gentlemen do not say straight out what they feel. That is all very well for grown-ups. You do like me, don't you?'

Although I was very pleased that she should be talking so frankly to me, still, I was a little hurt. I wished to show her that she was not dealing with a mere boy, and so, putting on as solemn a manner as I could, I said as casually as I was able: 'Of course I like you very much, Zinaida Alexandrovna. I have no wish to conceal it.'

She shook her head with deliberation. 'Have you a tutor?' she suddenly asked.

'No, I haven't had one for a long time.' This was a lie. Scarcely a month had passed since I had parted with my Frenchman.

'Yes, I see; you are quite grown up.' She rapped me lightly over the fingers.

'Hold your hands straight.' And she busily began to wind the ball of wool.

I took advantage of the fact that her eyes remained lowered, to scrutinize her features, at first stealthily and then more and more boldly. Her face appeared to me even more lovely than on the previous day. Everything in it was so delicate, clever and charming. She was sitting with her back to a window which was shaded by a white blind. A sunbeam filtering through the blind shed a gentle light on her soft golden hair, on her pure throat, on her tranquil breast. I gazed at her, and how dear she already was to me, and how near. It seemed to me that I had known her for a long time, and that before her I had known nothing and had not lived. . . . She was wearing a dark rather worn dress with an apron. How gladly would I have caressed every fold of that apron. The tips of her shoes looked out from under her skirt. I could have knelt in adoration to those shoes. 'And here I am sitting opposite her,' I was thinking, 'I have met her; I know her. God, what happiness!' I almost leapt from my chair in ecstasy, but in fact I only swung my legs a little, like a child enjoying a sweet. I was as happy as a fish in water.

I could have stayed in that room – I could have remained in it for ever.

Her eyes softly opened, and once more her clear eyes shone sweetly upon me, and again she gave me a gentle little smile.

'How you do stare at me,' she said slowly, and shook her finger.

I blushed. 'She understands everything; she sees everything,' flashed through my brain, and how could she fail to see it all and understand it all? Suddenly there was a sound from the next room – the clank of a sabre.

'Zina!' cried the old princess from the drawing-room. 'Byelovzorov has brought you a kitten.'

'A kitten,' cried Zinaida and, darting from her chair, threw the ball of wool into my lap, and ran out of the room. I, too, got up, left the skein of wool and the ball on the window-sill and stopped in amazement. In the middle of the room a small tabby cat was lying on its back, stretching out its paws. Zinaida was on her knees before it, cautiously lifting up its little face. By the side of the old princess, filling almost the entire space between the windows, stood a blond, curly-haired young officer, a magnificent figure with a pink face and protruding eyes.

'What a funny little thing,' Zinaida kept repeating, 'and its eyes aren't grey, they're green, and what large ears. I do thank you, Victor Yegorych. It is very sweet of you.'

The soldier, whom I recognized as one of the young men I had seen the evening before, smiled and bowed with a clink of his spurs and a jingle of his sabre rings.

'You were kind enough to say yesterday that you wanted a tabby kitten with large ears ... and here, you see, I have procured one. Your word is law.' And he bowed again.

The kitten uttered a feeble squeak and began to sniff the floor.

'It's hungry!' exclaimed Zinaida. 'Vonifaty, Sonia, bring some milk.'

The maid, in a shabby yellow dress, with a faded kerchief round her neck, came in with a saucer of milk in her hands, and set it before the kitten. The kitten started, screwed up its eyes, and began to lap.

'What a pink little tongue,' observed Zinaida, almost touching the floor with her head, and peering at the kitten sideways under its very nose. The kitten drank its fill and began to purr, delicately kneading with its paws. Zinaida rose, and turning to the maid said casually: 'Take it away'.

'In return for the kitten – your hand,' said the soldier with a simper and a great shrug of his powerful body tightly encased in a new uniform.

'Both of them,' Zinaida replied, and held out her hands to him. While he kissed them, she looked at me over his shoulder. I stood stock still and did not know whether to laugh, to say something, or to remain silent. Suddenly I saw through the open door in the hall, the figure of our footman, Fyodor. He was making signs to me. Mechanically I went out to him.

'What is the matter?' I asked.

'Your Mama has sent for you,' he replied in a whisper. 'Madam is annoyed because you haven't come back with the answer.'

'Why, have I been here long?'

'Over an hour.'

'Over an hour!' I repeated automatically, and returning to the drawing-room, I began to take my leave, bowing and clicking my heels.

'Where are you off to?' asked the young princess, glancing at me over the officer's back.

'I am afraid I must go home. So I am to say,' I added, turning to the old princess, 'that you will honour us at about two o'clock?'

'Yes, my dear sir, please say just that,' she said.

The old princess hastily reached for a snuff box and took the snuff so noisily that I almost jumped. 'That's right, say precisely that,' she wheezily repeated, blinking tearfully.

I bowed again, turned and walked out of the room with that uncomfortable sensation in my back which a very young man feels when he knows he is being watched from behind.

'Now, Monsieur Woldemar, mind you come and see us again,' cried Zinaida, and laughed once more.

Why is she always laughing, I thought, as I returned home, accompanied by Fyodor who said nothing to me, but walked behind me with a disapproving air. My mother scolded me and expressed surprise. Whatever could have kept me so long with the princess? I gave no answer and went off to my room. Suddenly, I felt extremely depressed ... I tried hard not to cry ... I was jealous of the soldier!

5

THE old princess, as she had promised, called on my mother who did not take to her. I was not present at their meeting, but at table my mother told my father that this Princess Zasyekin seemed to her *'une femme très vulgaire'*, that she had found her very tiresome, with her requests to do something for her with Prince Sergey; that she seemed to have endless lawsuits and affairs, *'des vilaines affaires d'argent'*, and that she must be a very troublesome woman. But my mother did add that she had asked her and her daughter to dinner next day (when I heard the words 'and her daughter' I buried my face in my plate) for she was, after all, a neighbour, and a titled one, too.

My father thereupon informed my mother that he now remembered who this lady was: that in his youth he had known the late Prince Zasyekin, a very well-bred, but empty and ridiculous man; he said that he was called *'le Parisien'* in society because he had lived in Paris for a long time; that he had been very rich, but had gambled away all his property, and then, for no known reason – it might even have been for money, though he might, even so, have chosen better, my father added with a cold smile – he married the daughter of some minor official and, after his marriage, had begun to speculate in a large way, and had finally completely ruined himself.

'I only hope she won't try to borrow money,' put in my mother.

'That is quite possible,' said my father calmly. 'Does she speak French?'

'Very badly.'

'H'mm. Anyway, that does not matter. I think you said you had asked the daughter too? Somebody was telling me that she is a very charming and cultivated girl.'

'Ah, she can't take after her mother, then.'

'No, nor after her father,' my father said. 'He was very cultivated too, but a fool.'

My mother sighed, and returned to her own thoughts. My father said no more. I felt very uncomfortable during this conversation.

After dinner, I went into the garden, but without a gun. I promised myself not to go near the Zasyekins' garden, but an uncontrollable force drew me thither – and not in vain. I had hardly reached the fence when I saw Zinaida. This time she was alone. She was walking slowly along the path, holding a book in her hands. She did not notice me. I very nearly let her pass by, but suddenly collected myself, and coughed. She turned round, but did not stop. With her hand she pushed back the broad blue ribbon of her round straw hat, looked at me, smiled gently, and again turned her gaze to the book.

I took off my cap and after shuffling a little, walked away with a heavy heart. *'Que suis-je pour elle?'* I thought (goodness knows why) in French.

I heard familiar footsteps behind me. I looked round and saw my father walking towards me with his quick, light step. 'Is that the young princess?' he asked me.

'It is.'

'Why, do you know her?'

'I saw her this morning in her mother's house.'

My father stopped, and, turning sharply on his heel, went back. When he drew level with Zinaida, he bowed politely to her. She also bowed, though she looked a trifle surprised, and lowered her book. I saw how she followed him with her eyes. My father always dressed with great distinction, simply, and with a style of his own, but never did his figure seem to me more elegant, never did his grey hat sit more handsomely upon his curly hair that was scarcely touched by time. I made as if to move towards Zinaida, but she did not even glance at me. She raised her book again, and walked away.

6

I SPENT the whole of that evening and the following morning in a kind of dumb and frozen misery. I remember I tried to work and opened Kaidanov, but the broadly spaced lines and pages of the celebrated textbook flitted past my eyes in vain. Ten times over I read to myself the words 'Julius Caesar was distinguished for military valour', understood nothing, and threw the book aside.

Before dinner I carefully pomaded my hair again, and again put on my little frock-coat and neck-tie.

'Why all this?' asked my mother. 'You are not at the university yet, and Heaven knows whether you will get through the examination. And your short jacket wasn't made so very long ago – you can't throw it away yet.'

'Visitors are coming,' I murmured, almost in despair.

'What nonsense! Visitors indeed!'

I had to give in. I replaced the jacket with a short coat, but did not take off the neck-tie.

The old princess and her daughter appeared half an hour before dinner. The old woman had put a yellow shawl over the green dress in which I had seen her before, and wore an old-fashioned bonnet with flame-coloured ribbons. She began talking at once about her debts and bills, moaning and complaining about her poverty; evidently she felt completely at ease. She took snuff as noisily as ever, and fidgeted and turned about on her chair as much as before. It never seemed to have entered her head that she was a princess.

On the other hand, Zinaida was very stiff, almost haughty – a real princess. Her face remained coldly immobile and solemn. I saw no trace of the glances and smile that I knew, although in this new aspect, too, she seemed to me very beautiful. She wore a light *barège* dress with pale blue flowers on it. Her hair fell in long curls down her cheeks in the English fashion. This style went well with the cold expression on her face. My father sat beside her during dinner, and entertained his neighbour with his usual calm and elegant courtesy. Now and then, he glanced at her, and from time to time she looked at him – but so strangely, almost with hostility. Their conversation was in French – I remember that I was surprised by the purity of Zinaida's accent.

During the meal, the old princess behaved as before, without ceremony, eating a great deal and praising the dishes. My mother obviously found her very tedious and replied to her with a kind of sad disdain. Now and then my father frowned a little.

My mother did not like Zinaida either. 'She seems terribly conceited,' she said on the next day. 'And what has she to be so very proud about, *avec sa mine de grisette*?'

'You've evidently never seen grisettes,' observed my father.

'No, thank God.'

26

'Yes, indeed, thank God; only in that case how can you have views about them?'

To me, Zinaida had pointedly paid not the slightest attention.

Soon after dinner the old princess began to take her leave.

'I shall hope for your kind aid and protection, Maria Nicolayevna and Pyotr Vassilitch,' she said in a sing-song to my mother and father. 'What can one do? Time was ... but it is over, and here I am, a princess' – and she added with a disagreeable laugh, 'a title's no good without any food!'

My father made an elaborate bow and accompanied her to the door of the hall. There I stood, in my short little jacket, staring at the floor like a prisoner condemned to death. Zinaida's treatment of me had utterly killed me. What then was my astonishment when, as she passed by me, her face wearing its former warm expression, she whispered quickly to me, 'Come and see us at eight o'clock, do you hear? Don't fail me.'

I threw up my hands, but already she was gone, flinging a white scarf round her head.

7

PUNCTUALLY at eight o'clock, in my frock-coat, and with my hair brushed into a coxcomb, I walked into the hall of the lodge where the old princess was living. The old servant gave me a sour look, and rose unwillingly from the bench.

The sound of gay voices reached me from the drawing-

27

room. I opened the door and stopped short in amazement. In the middle of the room on a chair stood the young princess, holding out a man's hat. Five young men clustered round the chair. They were trying to put their hands into the hat, but she kept it above their heads, shaking it violently every now and then. On seeing me, she cried, 'Stop, stop, another guest! We must give him a ticket, too!' and, leaping lightly from the chair, took me by the cuff of my coat.

'Come along,' she said, 'why are you all standing about? *Messieurs*, may I introduce you? This is M'sieu Woldemar, our neighbour's son, and these,' she added, turning to me and pointing to the guests as she named them, 'are Count Malevsky, Doctor Looshin, the poet Maidanov, retired Captain Nirmatsky, and Byelovzorov the hussar, whom you have seen already – you will all be friends, I hope.'

I was so acutely embarrassed that I did not even bow. In Dr Looshin I recognized the same swarthy man who had humiliated me so cruelly in the garden. The others I did not know.

'Count,' Zinaida continued, 'write out a ticket for M'sieu Woldemar.'

'That's not fair,' said the count, with a slight Polish accent. He was very handsome, with dark hair, expressive brown eyes, a small, narrow white nose and a thin little moustache over a tiny mouth, and was fashionably dressed. 'This gentleman did not take part in our game of forfeits.'

'It's not fair,' echoed Byelovzorov and the figure referred to as the retired captain, a man about forty, hideously pockmarked, with curly hair like a negro's, slightly bowed bandy legs, and wearing a military tunic, unbuttoned and without epaulettes.

'Write out the ticket, I tell you,' repeated the princess. 'What is this? A mutiny? M'sieu Woldemar is here for the first time, and today the rule does not apply to him. No grumbling; write out the ticket – that is my wish.'

The count shrugged his shoulders, but bowing his head obediently, took a pen in his white, beringed fingers, reached for a piece of paper and began to write.

'At least may I be allowed to explain to M'sieu Woldemar what this is all about?' Looshin began in a sarcastic voice. 'Otherwise he'll be quite lost. You see, young man, we are playing a game of forfeits. The princess has had to pay a forfeit and the winner, whoever draws the lucky ticket, will have the right to kiss her hand. Do you understand what I have just said?'

I only looked at him, and continued to stand there in a haze while the princess again leapt on to the chair, and once more began to shake the hat. Everyone moved towards her, I with the others.

'Maidanov,' said the princess to a tall young man with a thin face, small, short-sighted eyes and extremely long black hair, 'you, as a poet, should be magnanimous and yield your ticket to M'sieu Woldemar so that he may have two chances instead of one.' But Maidanov shook his head, tossing back his hair.

I was the last to put my hand into the hat, and, taking the ticket, opened it. Heavens! What did I feel when I saw upon it the word, 'Kiss'!

'Kiss!' I could not help crying out.

'Bravo, he wins,' the princess exclaimed. 'I am so pleased.'

She stepped down from the chair and looked into my eyes with a look so sweet and clear that my heart missed a beat. 'And are you pleased?' she asked me.

'I?' I stammered.

'Sell me your ticket,' blurted Byelovzorov suddenly into my ear. 'I will give you a hundred roubles.'

I gave the soldier a look so indignant that Zinaida clapped her hands and Looshin exclaimed, 'Oh, well done! But,' he added, 'I, as master of ceremonies, am obliged to see to it that all the rules are kept. Monsieur Woldemar, go down on one knee. That is the rule.'

Zinaida stood before me, with her head a little on one side, as if to see me better, and solemnly held out her hand to me. Everything became blurred. I meant to go down on one knee, but fell on both, and touched Zinaida's fingers so awkwardly with my lips that I scratched the tip of my nose on her nail.

'Splendid!' shouted Looshin, and helped me to get up.

The game continued. Zinaida put me next to herself, and what forfeits she thought of! She had, among other things, to represent a statue, and she chose the hideous Nirmatsky as her pedestal, told him to bend down and then to bury his face in his chest. The laughter never stopped for an instant. For me, brought up as I had been, a solitary boy in the sober atmosphere of a staid country house, all this noise and excitement, this uncontrolled gaiety, the queer new terms on which I found myself with these strangers, all went straight to my head: I felt intoxicated – it was like a strong wine.

I began to laugh and chatter more loudly than the others, so that even the old princess, who was sitting in the next room with some official from the Legal Department, who had been called in for consultation, actually came out to have a look at me. But I felt so immensely happy that I didn't care a rap. I really didn't care what mockery, or what cross looks were directed at me. Zinaida continued to favour me, and would not let me leave her side. For one forfeit I had to sit beside her, both of us under the same silk scarf; I was supposed to tell her 'my secret'. I remember how both our heads were suddenly plunged in a close, fragrant, almost transparent darkness, and how close to me in this darkness her eyes shone softly; and I remember the warm breath from her parted lips, the gleam of her teeth, and how her hair tickled and burnt me. I was silent. She smiled mysteriously and slyly, and finally whispered to me, 'Well?' But I only blushed and laughed and turned away, and could scarcely breathe.

We became bored with forfeits, and began playing 'String'. What joy I felt when, my attention wandering, I received a sharp, strong slap on my fingers, and how, afterwards, I tried on purpose to look as if I weren't paying attention and how she teased me and would not touch my outstretched hands! And the things we did that evening! We played the piano, we sang, we danced, we acted a gipsy camp. Nirmatsky was dressed up as a bear and made to drink salt water. Count Malevsky showed us various card tricks, and finished – after shuffling all the cards – by dealing himself a whist hand, all trumps, upon which Looshin 'had the honour to congratulate him'. Maidanov recited fragments from his poem *The Murderer* (this was at the height of the romantic period) which he intended to bring out in a black cover, with the title printed in blood-red letters. We stole the official's cap off his knee and made

31

him, as a ransom, dance a Cossack dance. We dressed up old Vonifaty in a bonnet, and the young princess put on a man's hat.... We went on endlessly.

Byelovzorov alone kept to his corner, scowling and glowering. Sometimes his eyes would become bloodshot, his face would turn red, and then he looked as if he might, at any moment, suddenly hurl himself at us and scatter us like chaff in all directions. But the princess would glance at him now and then, shake her finger, and he would once more retreat to his corner.

At last we were completely worn out. Even the old princess who, to use her own expression, could take anything (no amount of noise seemed to upset her) – even she began to feel a little tired and decided to go and rest. Towards midnight, supper was brought in. It consisted of a piece of stale, dry cheese and some sort of small cold ham patties, which seemed to me more delicious than any pasty. There was only one bottle of wine, and a very queer one at that. The bottle was dark, with a wide neck, and the wine inside was vaguely pink; in point of fact, no one drank it. Exhausted but happy, almost collapsing, I left the lodge. Zinaida pressed my hand as I left, and again smiled mysteriously.

The night air was raw and heavy against my burning face. A storm seemed to be gathering, the black thunder clouds grew and slowly crept across the sky, visibly changing their misty outlines; a light wind shuddered restlessly in the dark trees, and from somewhere far beyond the horizon came the muffled sound of thunder, as if muttering angrily to itself.

I crept to my room by the back stairs. My man was sleeping on the floor, and I had to step over him. He woke up, saw me, and reported that my mother had again been angry with me, and had again wished to send for me, but that my father had restrained her. (I never went to bed without saying goodnight to my mother, and asking her blessing.)

But there was nothing to be done! I told my man that I would undress and get myself to bed, and then I put out the candle. But I did not undress, and did not lie down. I sat down on a chair, and remained so for a long time, as if under a spell. What I felt was so new, so sweet. I sat quite still, hardly looking round, and breathing very slowly; only from time to time I laughed silently at some memory, or grew cold at the thought that I was in love – it was here – this was love. Zinaida's face swam gently before me in the darkness, floated, but did not float away. Her lips wore the same mysterious smile: her eyes looked at me, a little from one side, inquiring, tender, pensive, as she had looked when I left her.

At last I got up, tiptoed to my bed and, without undressing, laid my head carefully on the pillow, as if afraid of upsetting, by some sudden movement, that which filled my entire being.

I lay down, but did not even close my eyes. Soon I noticed feeble gleams of light constantly lighting the room. I sat up and looked at the window. The frame stood out sharply from the mysterious light of the panes. A storm, I thought, and I was right. A storm it was, very far away, so that the thunder could not be heard; only pale, long forks of lightning flashed ceaselessly across the sky; not flashing so much as quivering and twitching, like the wing of a dying bird.

I rose, went to the window, and stood there till

morning ... the lightning did not cease for an instant. It was what the peasants call a Sparrow Night. I looked at the silent, sandy stretch, at the dark mass of the Neskootchny Gardens, at the yellowish façades of distant buildings which seemed to quiver too, with each faint flash. I gazed, and could not tear myself away. This silent lightning, this controlled light, seemed to answer to the mute and secret fires which were blazing within me. Morning began to dawn. The sky was stained crimson. As the sun rose, the lightning became fainter and less frequent; the flashes came more and more seldom, and finally ceased, drowned in the clear and unambiguous light of the rising day. And the flashes within me died down too. I felt weary and at peace, but the image of Zinaida still hovered triumphant over my soul, though even this image seemed more tranquil. Like a swan rising from the grasses of the marsh, it stood out from the unlovely shapes which surrounded it, and I, as I fell asleep, in parting for the last time clung to it, in trusting adoration.

Oh, gentle feelings, soft sounds, the goodness and the gradual stilling of a soul that has been moved; the melting happiness of the first tender, touching joys of love – where are you? Where are you?

8

NEXT morning, when I came down to breakfast, my mother scolded me – not as much as I expected – and made me describe how I had spent the previous evening. I replied briefly, leaving out many details, and tried to make everything seem completely innocent.

'All the same, they are not at all *comme il faut*,' remarked my mother, 'and I wish you would not waste your time in such company, instead of doing some work for your examination.'

Knowing as I did that my mother's concern with my studies would be confined to these few words, I did not think it necessary to answer her; but after breakfast, my father put his arm through mine and, taking me into the garden, made me give him a full account of all I had seen at the Zasyekins'.

My father had a curious influence on me, and our relations were curious too. He took scarcely any interest in my education, but never hurt my feelings; he respected my freedom; he displayed – if one can put it that way – a certain courtesy towards me; only he never let me come at all close to him. I loved him, I was full of admiration for him; he seemed to me the ideal man – and God knows how passionately attached to him I should have been if I had not felt constantly the presence of his restraining hand. Yet he could, whenever he wished, with a single word, a single gesture, instantly make me feel complete trust in him. My soul would open; I chattered to him as to a wise friend, an indulgent mentor ... and then, just as suddenly, he would abandon me, his hand would again push me aside – kindly and gently – but, nevertheless, aside.

Sometimes a mood of gaiety would come over him, and at such moments he was ready to play and romp with me, full of high spirits like a boy. He loved all violent physical exercise.

Once, and only once, he caressed me with such tenderness that I nearly cried ... then his gaiety and tenderness vanished without a trace. But when this happened it never gave me any hope for the future – I seemed to have seen it all in a dream. At times I would watch his clear, handsome, clever face ... my heart would tremble, my entire being would yearn towards him ... then, as if he sensed what was going on within me he would casually pat my cheek – and would either leave me, or start doing something, or else would suddenly freeze as only he knew how. Instantly I would shrink into myself, and grow cold. His rare fits of affability towards me were never in answer to my own unspoken but obvious entreaties. They always came unexpectedly. When, later, I used to think about my father's character, I came to the conclusion that he cared nothing for me nor for family life; it was something very different he loved, which wholly satisfied his desire for pleasure. 'Take what you can yourself, and don't let others get you into their hands; to belong to oneself, that is the whole thing in life,' he said to me once. On another occasion, being at that time a youthful democrat, I embarked on a discussion of liberty in his presence (on that day he was what I used to call 'kind'; then one could talk about anything to him).

'Liberty,' he repeated. 'Do you know what really makes a man free?'

'What?'

'Will, your own will, and it gives power which is better than liberty. Know how to want, and you'll be free, and you'll be master too.'

Before and above everything, my father wanted to live ... and did live. Perhaps he had a premonition that he would not have long in which to make use of the 'thing in life'; he died at forty-two.

I gave my father a detailed account of my visit to the Zasyekins. Sitting on a bench he listened to me, half-attentively, half-absently – drawing in the sand with his riding-crop. From time to time he would laugh lightly, glance at me in an odd, bright, gay manner, and egg me on with short questions and rejoinders. At first I scarcely dared to pronounce Zinaida's name, but could not contain myself, and began to sing her praises. My father merely continued to smile; presently he became thoughtful, stretched himself, and rose.

I remembered that as he was leaving the house he had ordered his horse to be saddled. He was a superb rider and could break in the wildest horse long before Monsieur Rarey.

'Shall I come with you, Papa?' I asked.

'No,' he replied, and his face assumed its usual expression of benevolent indifference. 'Go alone, if you want to; and tell the coachman that I shall not be going.'

He turned his back on me, and walked quickly away. I followed him with my eyes. He disappeared behind the gate. I saw his hat moving along the hedge: he went into the Zasyekins' house.

He did not stay there more than an hour. Then he went straight off to the town and stayed away till evening.

After dinner I myself called on the Zasyekins. In the drawing-room I found only the old princess. When she saw me she scratched her head under her bonnet with a knitting needle and suddenly asked me whether I would copy out a petition for her.

'With pleasure,' I replied, and sat down on the edge of a chair.

'Only mind, make your letters nice and big,' said

the princess, handing me a badly scribbled sheet of paper.

'Could you do it today, my dear sir?'

'I will copy it today, ma'am.'

The door into the next room opened slightly. Through the gap Zinaida's face appeared – pale, pensive, her hair carelessly thrown back. She looked at me with large, cold eyes and softly closed the door.

'Zina, I say, Zina,' said the old woman. Zinaida did not respond. I took away the old woman's petition and sat the whole evening over it.

9

FROM that day my 'passion' began. What I experienced then, I remember, was something similar to what a man must feel when first given an official post. I had ceased to be simply a young boy; I was someone in love. I say that my passion began from that day; and I might add that my suffering began on that day too. In Zinaida's absence I pined: I could not concentrate: I could not do the simplest thing. For whole days I did nothing but think intensely about her. I pined away, but her presence brought me no relief. I was jealous and felt conscious of my worthlessness. I was stupidly sulky, and stupidly abject; yet an irresistible force drew me towards her, and it was always with an involuntary shiver of happiness that I went through the door of her room.

Zinaida guessed at once that I had fallen in love with her, but then I wouldn't have thought of concealing it. My passion amused her. She made fun of me, played with me, and tormented me. It is sweet to be the sole source, the arbitrary and irresponsible source of the greatest joys and profoundest miseries to someone else. I was like soft wax in the hands of Zinaida; not that I alone had fallen in love with her. All the men who visited the house were hopelessly infatuated, and she kept them all on leading-strings at her feet. She found it amusing to excite alternate hopes and fears in them; to twist them according to her whim. She called this, 'knocking people against each other'; they did not even think of resistance, but gladly submitted to her. In her whole being, vital and beautiful, there was a peculiarly fascinating mixture of cunning and insouciance, artifice and simplicity, gentleness and gaiety. Over everything she did and said, over every movement, there hovered a subtle, exquisite enchantment. Everything expressed the unique, peculiar force of the life which played within her. Her face, too, was constantly changing. It, too, was always in play. It seemed at almost the same instant mocking, pensive and passionate. An infinite variety of feelings, light and swift, succeeded each other like shadows of clouds on a windy summer day, in her eyes and on her lips. Every one of her admirers was necessary to her. Byelovzorov, whom she sometimes called 'my wild beast', or sometimes simply 'mine', would gladly have leapt into the fire for her. With no confidence in his own brains or other qualities, he was constantly proposing marriage to her, implying that the others only talked. Maidanov was responsive to the poetic strain in her soul; somewhat cold by nature, like nearly all writers, he assured her fervently, and perhaps himself too, that he adored her. He composed endless verses in her honour, and recited them with an ardour at once affected and sincere. She sympathized with him and, at the same

39

time, faintly mocked him. She did not really trust him, and after listening to his effusions for a while, used to make him read Pushkin, in order, as she used to say, to clear the air.

Looshin, the sarcastic doctor, so cynical in his talk, knew her best of all, and loved her more than the others, although he attacked her, both to her face and behind her back. She respected him, but did not spare him, and sometimes, with a peculiar malicious pleasure, used to make him feel her complete power over him. 'I am a flirt: I have no heart: I have an actor's nature,' she once said to him in my presence. 'All right then. Give me your hand and I will stick a pin into it, and you will feel ashamed in front of this young man. And it will hurt you, and still you will be kind enough to laugh, Mr Truthful.' Looshin flushed, turned away, bit his lip, but in the end stretched out his hand. She pricked it, and he did begin to laugh, and she laughed too, and drove the pin quite deep, and kept glancing into his eyes, which ran helplessly in every direction.

Least of all did I understand the relations which existed between Zinaida and Count Malevsky. He was good-looking, clever and shrewd, but something false in him, something equivocal, was apparent even to me, a boy of sixteen, and I wondered that Zinaida did not notice it. But perhaps she did notice this falseness and was not repelled by it. An irregular education, odd habits and company, the perpetual presence of her mother, poverty and disorder in the house – everything, beginning with the freedom which the young girl enjoyed, with her consciousness of superiority over her surroundings, had developed in her a curious, half-contemptuous kind of carelessness and unfastidiousness. I remember how, no matter what happened – whether Vonifaty announced there was no sugar left, or perhaps some squalid piece of gossip suddenly became public, or some quarrel broke out between the guests – she would only shake her curls and say, 'Fiddlesticks!' and leave it at that.

But my blood, I remember, used to rise when Malevsky would sidle up to her like a sly fox, lean gracefully over the back of her chair, and begin to whisper into her ear with a self-satisfied and wheedling little smile – while she would fold her arms and glance at him attentively, then smile herself and shake her head.

'What induces you to receive Monsieur Malevsky?' I once asked her.

'Ah, but he has such beautiful little moustaches,' she replied. 'And anyway that is not your province.'

'Perhaps you think that I love him?' she said to me on another occasion. 'No! I cannot love people whom I find that I look down on. I need someone who would himself master me, but then, goodness me, I shall never come across anyone like that. I will never fall into anybody's clutches, never, never.'

'Does that mean that you will never love anyone?'

'And what about you? Don't I love you?' she said, and flicked me on the nose with the tip of her glove.

Yes, Zinaida made fearful fun of me. For three weeks I saw her every day, and there was nothing that she didn't do to me. She called on us seldom, and about this I was not sorry. In our house, she became transformed into a young lady, a princess, and this made me shy of her. I was frightened of giving myself away to my mother. She did not think at all well of Zinaida, and watched us with disapproval. I was not so nervous of my father. He behaved as if he did not notice me, and did not say much to her. But what he did say seemed somehow specially wise and significant.

I ceased to work, to read, even to walk in the neighbourhood or to ride. Like a beetle tied by the leg, I circled constantly round the adored lodge. I felt I could have stayed there for ever, but this was not possible. My mother grumbled and sometimes Zinaida herself used to drive me away. Then I used to lock myself in my room, or go to the end of the garden, climb on to the ruin of a high stone greenhouse and, dangling my legs from the wall which looked out on the road, would sit for hours, staring and staring, seeing nothing. Near me, over the dusty nettles, white butterflies fluttered lazily. A pert little sparrow would fly down on to a half-broken red brick nearby, and would irritate me with its chirping, ceaselessly turning its whole body with its outspread tail; the crows, still wary, occasionally cawed, sitting high, high on the bare top of a birch – while the sun and wind played gently in its spreading branches; the bells of the Donskoy monastery would sometimes float across – tranquil and sad – and I would sit and gaze and listen, and would be filled with a nameless sensation which had everything in it: sorrow and joy, a premonition of the future, and desire, and fear of life. At the time, I understood none of this, and could not have given a name to any of the feelings which seethed within me; or else I would have called it all by one name – the name of Zinaida.

And Zinaida still played with me like a cat with a mouse. Sometimes she flirted with me – and that would excite me, and I would melt. At other times, she would

42

suddenly push me away – and then I dared not approach her, dared not look at her. I remember once that she was very cold with me for several days. I was completely unnerved – I would hurry timidly into the lodge and then, like a coward, I would stay with the old princess, in spite of the fact that she was particularly noisy and querulous at this time. Her financial affairs were going badly, and she had already had two encounters with the local police.

Once I was in the garden when, passing the well-known hedge, I saw Zinaida; leaning back on both her arms, she was sitting motionless on the grass. I was about to tiptoe away, but she suddenly raised her head and beckoned to me imperiously. I stood transfixed. I did not understand at once. She repeated the gesture. Immediately I leaped over the hedge and ran up to her happily, but she stopped me with a glance and pointed to a path two steps away from her. In confusion, and not knowing what to do, I went down on my knees on the edge of the path. She was so pale, every feature betrayed such bitter grief, such utter exhaustion that I felt a pang and murmured involuntarily, 'What is the matter?'

Zinaida stretched out her hand, plucked a blade of grass, bit it, and flung it away from her.

'Do you love me very much?' she asked at last. 'Do you?'

I did not reply – and indeed what reason had I to reply?

'Yes!' she said, looking at me as before, 'it is so. The same eyes – ' she added; then became thoughtful and covered her face with her hands. 'Everything has become horrible to me,' she whispered, 'why don't I go to the other end of the world! I can't bear it, I can't make it come right ... and what is there before me? ... God, I am so wretched!'

'Why?' I asked timidly.

Zinaida did not reply, but only shrugged her shoulders. I went on kneeling and looking at her with infinite distress. Every one of her words pierced my heart like a knife. At that moment I would, I think, gladly have given up my life if only that could end her grief. I looked at her, and still not understanding why she was so unhappy, conjured a vivid image of how, suddenly, in a paroxysm of ungovernable grief, she had walked into the garden and fallen to the ground as though mown down. All round us it was bright and green. The wind murmured in the leaves of the trees, now and then bending the raspberry canes above Zinaida's head. Somewhere doves were cooing and bees were buzzing, flying low from blade to blade over the sparse grass. Overhead, the sky was blue and tender, but I felt terribly sad.

'Read me some poetry,' said Zinaida in a low voice, and raised herself on one elbow. 'I like your reading poetry. You speak it in a sing-song, but I do not mind it, that's youth. Read me *On Georgia's Hills*, only first sit down.'

I sat down, and recited *On Georgia's Hills*.

'"Which it cannot help but love",' Zinaida repeated after me. 'That is what poetry can do. It speaks to us of what does not exist, which is not only better than what exists, but even more like the truth. "Which it cannot help but love" – it would like not to, but cannot help itself!' She was silent again and suddenly started and stood up. 'Let's go. Maidanov is with Mama. He has brought me his poem, but I left him. He is hurt too, now, but what can one do? One day you will discover ... only don't be angry with me.'

She pressed my hand hastily and moved quickly forward. We went back to the lodge.

Maidanov began to recite to us his recently published *Murderer*, but I did not listen. He shouted his four-foot iambics in a kind of sing-song. The rhymes succeeded each other, ringing like sleigh bells, hollow and shrill, while I could only look at Zinaida, trying to grasp the meaning of her last words.

> Or perchance it was some secret rival
> That sudden cast his spell on thee

exclaimed Maidanov suddenly in a nasal tone, and my eyes and Zinaida's met. She lowered hers and blushed slightly. I saw her blush and froze with terror. I was jealous of her before, but only at that instant did the thought that she was in love flash through my mind: 'My God, she has fallen in love!'

10

FROM that moment, my real torment began. I racked my brain, I thought of every possibility, and kept a ceaseless though, as far as possible, secret watch on Zinaida. A change had come over her, that was evident. She began to go for long, solitary walks. Sometimes she refused to see her visitors. For hours she sat alone in her room. She had never done this before. I suddenly developed – or it seemed to me that I had developed – tremendous perspicacity.

'Is it he? Or maybe it is not,' I used to ask myself,

anxiously running over in my mind one admirer after another. I secretly looked upon Count Malevsky (although it made me ashamed of Zinaida to admit this) as more dangerous than the others.

I could not see further than the end of my nose, and probably my secretiveness deceived no one. At any rate, Dr Looshin soon saw through me. Incidentally, he too had altered during this time. He had grown thinner, and though he laughed just as much, his laughter had somehow become shorter, more hollow, more malicious. Where previously there had been light irony and an affectation of cynicism, there was now a nervous irritability which he could not control.

'Why are you always trailing in and out of here, young man?' he once said to me when we were alone in the Zasyekins' drawing-room. The young princess had not returned from her walk. The shrill voice of the old lady resounded on the first floor. She was squabbling with her maid. 'You should be studying, working – while you are young – instead of which, you are doing what?'

'You can't tell whether I work at home or not,' I replied not without arrogance, but also in some confusion.

'A lot of work you do! You've something else on your mind. Oh, well, I won't argue ... at your age that is natural enough, but your choice isn't very fortunate. Can't you see what sort of house this is?'

'I don't quite understand,' I said.

'Don't understand? So much the worse for you. I consider it my duty to warn you. It is all very well for people like me – for old bachelors – to go on coming here. What could possibly happen to us? We are a hard-boiled lot; you cannot do much to us. But you have a tender skin. The atmosphere isn't healthy for you here. Believe me, you might become infected.'

'What do you mean?'

'What I say. Are you well now? Are you in a normal condition? Do you consider that what you feel now is healthy, is good for you?'

'Why, what am I feeling?' I said, knowing in my heart that the doctor was right.

'Ah, young man, young man,' the doctor went on, looking as if these two words contained something very insulting to me, 'it is no good trying that kind of thing on me. Why, bless you, whatever is in your heart is still written all over your face. But anyway, what is the good of talking? I shouldn't be coming here myself if – ' the doctor clenched his teeth, 'if I were not just as mad myself. Only what does astonish me is this; how can you with your intelligence not see what is going on round you?'

'Why, what *is* going on?' I rejoined, all on edge.

The doctor looked at me with a kind of mocking pity.

'But there's not much to be said for me either,' he said, as if to himself. 'In a word,' he added, raising his voice, 'I repeat, the atmosphere here is bad for you. You like it here – well, what of it? Hothouses smell sweet too, but one can't live in them. Take my advice and go back to Kaidanov again.'

The old princess came in and began to complain to the doctor about her toothache. Then Zinaida appeared.

'There,' finished the old princess. 'You must tell her off. She drinks iced water the whole day long. Now can that be good for her, with her weak chest?'

'Why do you do this?' asked Looshin.

'Why, what can it do to me?'

47

'Do to you? You could catch cold and die.'

'Really? Well, then that would be that.'

'Really? I see, so that's how it is,' grunted the doctor. The old princess left the room.

'Yes, that's how it is,' repeated Zinaida. 'Is life so gay then? Why, if you look around you ... well, is it so very attractive? Do you think that I don't understand, don't feel it? I get pleasure from drinking water with ice, and can you seriously maintain to me that this kind of life is not worth risking for a moment's pleasure? I don't speak of happiness.'

'Yes, I see,' said Looshin. 'Caprice and independence, the whole of you is contained in these two words. Your entire nature is conveyed by them.'

Zinaida gave a nervous laugh. 'You've missed the post, my dear doctor. You're not a good observer. You're too late. Put on your spectacles. This is no time for whims. Make a fool of yourself, make a fool of me ... the more the merrier. As for being independent – Monsieur Woldemar,' Zinaida added suddenly, stamping her foot, 'don't try to look so sad. I cannot bear to be pitied,' and she left us quickly.

'It is bad, bad for you, the atmosphere here, young man,' said Looshin again.

I I

THAT same evening there were the usual guests at the Zasyekins'. I was among them. Maidanov's poem was discussed. Zinaida praised it with complete sincerity.

'But I will tell you something,' she said to him. 'If I

48

were a poet, I would take quite different subjects. Perhaps this is all nonsense, but strange thoughts sometimes come into my head, particularly when I cannot sleep just before morning, when the sky begins to grow pink and grey. I should, for example – you won't laugh at me?'

'No, no,' we all cried with one voice.

'I would,' she continued, crossing her arms and gazing away, 'I would depict a whole company of young girls in a large boat on a quiet river at night. The moon is shining; they are all in white with wreaths of white flowers, and they are singing – you know, something like a hymn.'

'I understand, I understand; continue,' said Maidanov, in a meaningful and dreamy tone.

'Suddenly there is noise, loud laughter, torches, timbrels on the bank. It is a Bacchic rout singing and shouting along the riverside. Now it is your business to paint the picture, Sir Poet, only I want the torches to be red and very smoky, and I want the eyes of the Bacchantes to gleam under their wreaths, and the wreaths of flowers must be dark, and don't forget the tiger skins and the goblets and the gold – lots of gold.'

'Where is the gold to be?' asked Maidanov, throwing back his long hair and dilating his nostrils.

'Where? On their shoulders, arms, legs, everywhere. They say that in the ancient world women wore gold rings on their ankles. The Bacchantes call to the girls in the boat. The girls have ceased to sing their hymn. They cannot continue it, but they do not stir. The river is carrying them towards the bank. And then suddenly, one of them softly rises. This must be beautifully described. How she rises softly in the moonlight and how frightened

49

her friends are. She has stepped over the edge of the boat. The Bacchantes have surrounded her, and whirled her off into the night, into the dark. Here you must paint the swirling clouds of smoke and everything in chaos. Only their cries can be heard, and her wreath is left lying on the bank.'

Zinaida ceased. (Ah, she is in love, I thought again.)

'And is that all?' asked Maidanov.

'All!' she replied.

'That cannot be the subject for an entire poem,' he said pompously, 'but I shall make use of your idea for a lyric.'

'In the romantic style?' asked Malevsky.

'Yes, of course in the romantic style. The Byronic.'

'In my opinion Hugo is better than Byron,' carelessly threw out the young count. 'More interesting.'

'Hugo is a first-rate writer,' replied Maidanov, 'and my friend Tonkosheyev, in his Spanish novel *El Trovador* ...'

'Oh, is that the book with the question marks upside down?' Zinaida interrupted.

'Yes, that is the rule in Spanish. I was going to say that Tonkosheyev ...'

'Oh, you are going to have another argument about classicism and romanticism,' Zinaida interrupted him again. 'Let's play a game instead.'

'Forfeits?' said Looshin.

'No, forfeits are boring. Let's play analogies.' (Zinaida had invented this game herself. An object would be named, and everyone tried to compare it with something else. The person who thought of the best analogy won the prize.) She walked to the window. The sun had just set. Long red clouds stood high in the sky.

'What are those clouds like?' asked Zinaida, and without waiting for our answer said: 'I think they are like those purple sails on the golden ship in which Cleopatra sailed to meet Antony. Do you remember, Maidanov? You were telling me about it not long ago.'

All of us, like Polonius in *Hamlet*, decided that the clouds reminded us of precisely those sails, and that none of us could find a better analogy.

'How old was Antony then?' asked Zinaida.

'Oh, he must surely have been young,' observed Malevsky.

'Yes, young,' Maidanov agreed confidently.

'I beg your pardon,' exclaimed Looshin, 'he was over forty.'

'Over forty,' repeated Zinaida, giving him a quick glance.

I went home soon after. 'She is in love,' my lips whispered involuntarily, 'but with whom?'

12

THE days were passing. Zinaida grew stranger and stranger, more and more unaccountable. One day I went to see her and found her sitting on a wicker chair with her head pressed against the sharp edge of the table. She drew herself up ... her whole face was wet with tears.

'Ah! You!' she said with a cruel smile. 'Come here.'

I went up to her. She placed her hand on my head, suddenly seized me by the hair, and began to twist it.

'It hurts,' I said at last.

51

'Ah, it hurts, does it? And do you think it doesn't hurt me? Doesn't hurt me?' she repeated.

'Ai!' she cried suddenly, when she saw she had pulled out a small lock of my hair. 'What *have* I done? Poor M'sieu Woldemar.'

She carefully straightened the torn lock, curled it round her finger and twisted it into a little ring.

'I shall put your hair in my locket and I shall wear it,' she said, and her eyes were still full of tears. 'This will perhaps comfort you a little ... And now, good-bye.'

I returned home to find a disagreeable state of affairs. My mother was trying to 'have things out' with my father. She was reproaching him for something, and he, as was his habit, answered with polite and frigid silences, and soon went away. I could not hear what my mother was saying, nor was I in a mood to listen. I remember only that when the scene was over, she sent for me to the study, and spoke with great disapproval about my frequent visits to the old princess who, in her words, was *une femme capable de tout*. I bowed to kiss her hand (I always did this when I wanted to end a conversation) and went up to my room.

Zinaida's tears were altogether too much for me. I simply didn't know what to think and was on the point of tears myself. I was after all still a child, in spite of my sixteen years. I no longer thought about Malevsky, though Byelovzorov every day glared more and more savagely at the wily count, like a wolf at a sheep. But then, I had no thought for anything or anybody. I gave myself up to fruitless speculation, and was always looking for secluded places. I became particularly fond of the ruined greenhouse. I used to climb, I remember, on to the high wall, settle myself on it and sit there, a youth afflicted by such misery, solitude and grief that I would be overcome with self-pity. How I revelled in these melancholy feelings – how I adored them.

One day I was sitting on the wall staring into space, and listening to the bells chiming. Suddenly something went through me, softer than the gentlest puff of wind, scarcely a shiver, like a scarcely perceptible breath, the sense of someone's presence. I looked down. Below – on the road – in a light grey dress, with a pink parasol resting on her shoulder, Zinaida was walking quickly. She saw me, stopped, and turning back the brim of her straw hat, she lifted her velvet eyes towards me.

'What are you doing so high up there?' she asked me with an odd smile. 'Now you always declare,' she went on, 'that you love me. Well, then, jump down into the road to me, if you truly love me.'

Hardly had Zinaida spoken these words when I was falling through the air, just as if someone had pushed me from behind. The wall was about fourteen feet high. I touched the ground with my feet, but the impact was so strong that I could not keep my balance. I fell flat and for an instant lost consciousness. When I came to, still without opening my eyes, I felt Zinaida near me.

'My darling boy,' she was saying, bending over me, and her voice was full of tender anxiety. 'How could you do it? How could you listen to me? When you know I love you . . . Oh, please stand up.'

Her bosom rose and fell beside me; her hands were touching my head and suddenly – oh, what became of me then? – her soft fresh lips began to cover my face with kisses. She touched my lips, but then Zinaida probably realized from the expression on my face that I had regained consciousness, although I still kept my eyes closed, and rising quickly, she said: 'Come, get up, you naughty boy, you idiot. Why are you lying in the dust?'

I got up.

'Give me my parasol,' said Zinaida. 'See where I have thrown it. Don't look at me like that – it is too ridiculous. You aren't hurt, are you? Stung by the nettles, I expect... I tell you, don't look at me ... why, he doesn't understand a word, he doesn't answer,' she said, as if to herself. 'Go home, Monsieur Woldemar, and tidy yourself up, and don't you dare follow me, or I shall be furious, and will never again...'

She did not finish her sentence, and moved quickly away. I sank down on the road. My legs would not carry me. My arms were smarting from the nettles, my back ached, my head swam, but at that moment I experienced a sense of bliss such as I never again felt in the whole of my life. It flowed like a delicious pain through all my limbs and finally resolved itself in rapturous leaps and cries. Yes, indeed, I was still a child.

13

I FELT so gay and proud all that day. I retained so vividly the sensation of Zinaida's kisses on my face – I recollected her every word with such ecstasy of delight, I nursed my unexpected happiness so tenderly, that I even suffered moments of anxiety in which I would actually have preferred never to see again the author of these new sensations. It seemed to me that there was nothing more I could ask of fate, that one might now 'go, take a deep, sweet, final breath and die'. And yet, on the next day, when I made my way to the lodge, I felt great embarrassment which I tried vainly to conceal by putting on the kind of modest yet quietly self-assured expression of someone who wished to convey that he can keep a secret. Zinaida received me very simply, without the slightest emotion. She merely shook her finger at me and asked whether I wasn't black and blue all over. All my modest self-assurance and air of mystery instantly dissolved, and with them my embarrassment. I did not, of course, expect anything extraordinary, but Zinaida's calm was like a cold douche. I realized that I was a child in her eyes, and my heart sank. Zinaida walked up and down in the room, giving me a quick smile every time she glanced at me; but her thoughts were far away – that I saw clearly.

Shall I begin about yesterday myself, I thought, and ask her where she was hurrying, and find out once and for all? ... But I couldn't; I let it pass, and humbly sat down in a corner.

Byelovzorov came in; I felt glad to see him.

'I've not managed to find you a quiet horse,' he said gruffly. 'Freitag says he absolutely guarantees one, but I don't feel safe – I feel afraid.'

'Afraid of what, may I ask?' said Zinaida.

'Of what? Why, you don't know how to ride. I dare not think of what might happen. What is this whim that's come into your head suddenly?'

'Ah, that's my own affair, Sir Beast. In that case I will ask Pyotr Vassilievich ...' (My father's name was Pyotr Vassilievich. I was astonished by her light, easy way of using his name – as if she were very certain of his readiness to do her a service.)

'I see,' retorted Byelovzorov, 'it's him you mean to go riding with?'

'With him – or someone else – that can't make any difference to you. Not with you, anyway.'

'Not with me,' Byelovzorov repeated, 'as you wish. Oh, well, I shall find a horse for you.'

'Very well. But don't go and get me an old cow: I warn you, I want to gallop.'

'Gallop as much as you want ... Who is it then, is it Malevsky you want to go riding with?'

'And why not he, Sir Warrior? Now, now, calm yourself,' she added, 'and don't glare so. I'll take you too. You know that for me Malevsky is now – fie! –' and she shook her head.

'You only say that to console me,' growled Byelovzorov.

Zinaida puckered her brow. 'Does that console you? Oh ... oh ... oh ... The Warrior!' she said finally, as if unable to find another word – 'and you, M'sieur Woldemar, would you come with us?'

'I am not fond ... a large company ...' I muttered without raising my eyes.

'Oh, you prefer a tête-à-tête? Well, freedom to the free, heaven for the holy,' she uttered with a sigh. 'Off you go, Byelovzorov, and do something. I must have a horse for tomorrow.'

'And where's the money to come from?' the old princess broke in.

Zinaida frowned. 'I am not asking you for it; Byelovzorov will trust me.'

'Trust you, trust you,' growled the old woman, and then suddenly screamed at the top of her voice, 'Doonyashka!'

'Maman, I have given you a little bell,' Zinaida put in.

'Doonyashka!' cried the old woman again.

Byelovzorov took his leave; I left with him ... Zinaida made no attempt to detain me.

14

NEXT day I rose early, cut myself a stick, and went off beyond the town gate. Perhaps a walk would dissipate my sorrows. It was a beautiful day, bright and not too hot, a gay, fresh wind was gently wandering over the earth; playing and softly murmuring, it touched everything lightly, disturbing nothing.

For a long time I wandered over the hills and in the woods. I did not feel happy – I had started with the set purpose of giving myself up to gloomy reflections. But youth, the beauty of the day, the freshness of the air, the pleasure which comes from rapid walking, the delicious sensation of lying on thick grass far away from everyone, alone – all these proved too strong. The memory of those unforgettable words, of those kisses, once more pierced into my soul. I thought with a certain pleasure that Zinaida could not, after all, fail to recognize my resolution, my heroism ... Others please her better than I, I thought; let them! But then others only speak of what they will do – whereas I have done it ... And that's nothing to what I can still do for her!

I saw a vision of myself saving her from the hands of

her enemies; I imagined how, covered with blood, I tore her from the very jaws of some dark dungeon and then died at her feet. I remembered the picture which used to hang in our drawing-room: Malek-Adel carrying off Matilda ... and then my attention was absorbed by the appearance of a large, brightly coloured woodpecker, busily climbing up the slender stem of a birch tree, and peering nervously from behind it, alternately to the right and to the left, like a double bass player from behind the neck of his instrument.

After this I sang *Not white the snows* which presently turned into the song well known at that time *For thee I wait when zephyrs wanton*; then I began to declaim Yermak's apostrophe to the stars from Khomyakov's tragedy; tried to compose something myself in the sentimental style – even getting so far as to think of the concluding line of the entire poem: '. . . Oh Zinaida! Zinaida!' but in the end made nothing of it.

In the meanwhile dinner-time was approaching, and I wandered down into the valley; a narrow sandy path wound its way through it towards the town. I walked along this path . . . The dull thud of horses' hooves sounded behind me. I looked round, stopped almost automatically, and took off my cap. I saw my father and Zinaida. They were riding side by side. My father was saying something to her; he was bending across towards her from the waist, with his hand propped on the neck of his horse; he was smiling. Zinaida listened to him in silence, her eyes firmly lowered, her lips pursed tightly. At first I saw only them; a few seconds later Byelovzorov came into view, in a hussar's uniform with a pelisse, on a foaming black horse. The noble animal tossed its head, pranced, snorted, while the rider at the same time held it back and spurred it on. I moved to one side, out of their way. My father gathered up the reins, and leant back away from Zinaida; she slowly lifted her eyes towards him, and they galloped off.

Byelovzorov raced after them, his sabre rattling. He is red as a lobster, I thought, she – why is she so pale? Out riding the whole morning – and yet so pale?

I walked twice as fast and got home just before dinner. My father was already sitting beside my mother's chair, washed and fresh and dressed for dinner, and was reading aloud to her, in his even, musical voice, the feuilleton from the *Journal des Débats*. But my mother listened to him without attention, and when she saw me asked what I had been doing with myself all day long, adding that she didn't like it when people went off God knows where and with God knows whom. 'But I was out for a walk, quite alone,' I was about to say, but glanced at my father, and for some reason remained silent.

15

DURING the next five or six days I hardly saw Zinaida at all; she declared herself unwell which, however, did not prevent the *habitués* of the lodge from dancing attendance upon her, as they put it; all except Maidanov, who instantly became bored and gloomy whenever there was no excuse for rapture. Byelovzorov sulked in a corner, all buttoned up and red-faced; over the delicate features of Count Malevsky there often hovered a malignant little smile; he really had fallen out of favour with Zinaida and was now waiting upon the old princess with exceptional assiduity; he accompanied her in a hired carriage when she paid a visit to the Governor-General. Actually this expedition turned out to be a failure and involved a dis-agreeable experience for Malevsky: an old scandal in-volving some sapper officers was brought up against him, and he had to explain it away by pleading his inexperience at the time. Looshin used to come once or twice a day but did not stay long; I was a little frightened of him after our last open conversation – yet at the same time I felt genuinely attracted to him. One day he went for a walk with me in the Neskootchny, was very amiable and agree-able, told me about the names and properties of various plants and flowers, when suddenly – it was really neither here nor there – he struck himself on the forehead and cried, 'And I, like a fool, thought that she was a flirt! Evidently to sacrifice oneself is the height of bliss – for some people!'

'What are you trying to say?' I asked.

'To you I am not trying to say anything,' Looshin brusquely replied.

Zinaida avoided me: my presence – I could not help noticing it – was disagreeable to her. Involuntarily she turned away from me ... involuntarily; it was that which was so bitter, so crushing – but there was nothing I could do. I did my best to keep out of her sight, and would try to watch her from a distance, which was not always possible.

As before, something was happening to her which I could not fathom: her face had altered: she became an entirely different being. The change which had taken place

60

in her struck me with peculiar force one warm, still evening, as I was sitting on a low seat under a spreading elder bush. I loved this corner of the garden: from it I could see the window of Zinaida's room. I sat there: in the dark mass of leaves over my head a small bird was rummaging about busily; a grey cat, its back stretched out, was creeping cautiously into the garden; the air, still clear but bright no longer, was heavy with the droning of the early beetles. I sat there, and looked at her window and waited in case it opened – and it did open, and Zinaida stood before me. She was wearing a white dress – and she was pale herself, her face, her shoulders, her arms were pale, almost white. She stood for a long time motionless, gazing straight before her with unmoving eyes, from under heavily knitted brows. Such a look I had never known upon her face. Then she clasped her hands tight, very tight, raised them to her lips – her forehead – then suddenly wrenched her fingers apart and thrust back her hair from her temples, tossed it; then with an air of resolution nodded, and shut the window with a slam.

Three days later she met me in the garden. I was on the point of moving away when she stopped me herself.

'Give me your hand,' she said, in the old caressing manner. 'We haven't had a gossip for a long time.'

I looked up at her: her eyes shone with a soft radiance, her face was smiling as if through a mist.

'Are you still unwell?' I asked her.

'No – it's all over now,' she answered and plucked a small red rose. 'I am a little tired, but that will pass.'

'And you will be the same as you were before?' I asked.

Zinaida lifted the rose to her face and it seemed to

61

me as if her cheeks caught the reflection of its bright petals.

'Why, am I changed then?' she asked.

'Yes, you are,' I answered in a low voice.

'I have been cold to you, I know,' began Zinaida, 'but you should not have taken any notice of it. I couldn't help it . . . but then, why talk about it?'

'You don't want me to love you – that's what it is!' I burst out gloomily, against my will.

'No. Love me, yes, but not as before.'

'Why, what am I to do?'

'Let us be friends – that's what.' Zinaida gave me the rose to smell. 'Listen, I am, after all, much older than you, I really might be your aunt – oh, well, perhaps not aunt, but elder sister. And you . . .'

'I am a child to you,' I interrupted.

'Well, yes, a child, but a sweet, good, clever child, whom I love very much. I'll tell you what. As from today you are appointed to be my page: and always remember that pages must never leave their mistress's side. And here is the token of your new dignity,' she added, putting the rose in the buttonhole of my jacket, 'a sign of our gracious favour.'

'I have received other favours from you before,' I murmured.

'Ah,' said Zinaida, and gave me a sidelong look. 'What a memory he has. Oh, well, I am just as ready now . . .' and bent down towards me and placed on my forehead a pure, calm kiss.

I did not look at her – she turned away and, saying 'Follow me, my page,' went towards the lodge. I walked behind her – and could not understand it. Can this gentle, sensible girl, I kept thinking, be the Zinaida whom I used to know?

Her very walk seemed gentler, her whole figure more stately and more graceful. Great Heavens! With what fresh force my love flamed up within me!

16

AFTER dinner the party gathered again at the lodge – and the young princess came down to them. The party was there in full force, as on that first, to me unforgettable, evening. Even Nirmatsky brought himself to attend: this time Maidanov arrived before anyone else – with some new verses. They played forfeits again, but this time without the eccentricities and the foolery and noise of the earlier occasion; the gipsy element had gone.

Zinaida gave the evening a different mood. I sat beside her, as her page. In the course of the evening she proposed that whoever had to pay a forfeit should tell his dream; but this was not a success. The dreams were either boring (Byelovzorov had dreamt that he had fed carp to his mare and that she had a wooden head), or were unnatural and too obviously made up. Maidanov treated us to a full-blown romantic tale, complete with sepulchres, angels with lyres, talking flowers, and sounds of music floating from afar. Zinaida did not let him finish.

'If we are to have made-up stories,' she said, 'then let everyone quite definitely invent something and tell us that.'

Byelovzorov again was obliged to begin. The young

hussar was acutely embarrassed. 'I can't think of anything to say,' he cried.

'What nonsense!' Zinaida caught him up. 'Can't you imagine, let us say, that you are married, and tell us how you would arrange your life with your bride. Would you lock her up?'

'I should.'

'And you would remain with her yourself?'

'Certainly. I should certainly stay with her all the time.'

'Admirable. And if this happened to bore her, and she deceived you?'

'I should kill her.'

'And if she ran away?'

'I should pursue and catch her and still kill her.'

'I see. And supposing that I were your wife, what would you do then?'

Byelovzorov, after a silence, said, 'I should kill myself.'

Zinaida began to laugh. 'I see your tale is quickly told.'

The next forfeit was Zinaida's.

She looked up at the ceiling and sat thinking.

'Listen,' she began at last, 'this is what I have thought of. Imagine a magnificent palace, a summer night, and a wonderful ball. The ball is being given by a young queen. Everywhere gold, marble, crystal, silk, lights, jewels, flowers, burning incense, every extravagance of luxury.'

'You like luxury?' Looshin interjected.

'Luxury is full of loveliness,' she rejoined. 'I adore all that is lovely.'

'More than the beautiful?' he asked.

'That sounds too clever – I don't understand it. Don't interrupt. Well then, the ball is magnificent. There are many guests. They are all young, beautiful, brave, and all are madly in love with the queen.'

'Are there no women among the guests?' asked Malevsky.

'No, or wait – there are.'

'All ugly?'

'No, ravishing – but the men are all in love with the queen. She is tall and graceful; upon her dark locks is set a small diadem of gold.'

I looked at Zinaida; and at that moment she seemed so high above us all; such luminous intelligence, such power shone from her calm white brow that I thought, 'You are your own story-queen.'

'They all throng about her,' Zinaida continued, 'they make speeches of fulsome flattery to her.'

'And she likes flattery?' Looshin asked.

'How insufferable he is; he will interrupt all the time . . . And who doesn't like flattery?'

'Just one last question,' put in Malevsky, 'has the queen a husband?'

'Why, I hadn't thought about that. No, why a husband?'

'Of course,' echoed Malevsky, 'why indeed?'

'*Silence!*' exclaimed Maidanov in French, which he spoke badly.

'*Merci,*' said Zinaida to him.

'And so the queen listens to their speeches, hears the music, but does not glance at any of the guests. Six windows are open from floor to ceiling and beyond them a dark sky with large stars and a dark garden with huge trees. The queen gazes into the garden. There, near the trees, is a fountain; it is white in the darkness and tall,

tall as a ghost. The queen hears, through the talk and the music, the soft plashing of its waters. She looks and thinks, You, Sirs, you are all noble, clever, rich, you throng round me, every one of my words is precious to you, you are all ready to die at my feet, you are my slaves ... But there, by the fountain, by the plashing water, he whose slave I am awaits me. He wears neither gorgeous raiment nor precious stones, no one knows him, but he awaits me, sure that I shall come – and I *shall* come – and there is no power in the world that can stop me when I want to go to him, to be with him, to lose myself with him there in the darkness of the garden, with the rustling of the trees and the murmur of the fountain ...' Zinaida was silent.

'And is this – fiction?' Malevsky asked craftily.

Zinaida did not even look at him.

'And what should we have done, gentlemen,' began Looshin suddenly, 'if we had been among the guests and had known about this fortunate man by the fountain?'

'Wait, wait,' Zinaida intervened, 'I will myself tell you how you would each have behaved. You, Byelovzorov, would have challenged him to a duel: you, Maidanov, would have perpetrated an epigram against him – or no, you don't know how to write epigrams, you would have written a long poem in iambics in the style of Barbier and would have got it into the *Telegraph*. You, Nirmatsky, would have borrowed – no, you would have lent him money at interest; you, doctor ...' she stopped. 'Now about you, I don't know what you would have done ...'

'Acting in my capacity of court physician,' answered

66

Looshin, 'I should have advised the queen not to give balls when she was not in the mood for guests.'

'Perhaps you would have been right. And you, Count?'

'And I?' echoed Malevsky with his malevolent little smile.

'You would have offered him a poisoned sweet.'

Malevsky's face gave a little quiver and for an instant took on a Jewish expression, but he at once let out a loud laugh.

'As for you, Woldemar,' Zinaida continued. 'However, that's enough; let's play another game.'

'M'sieu Woldemar, as the queen's page, would have carried her train as she ran into the garden,' Malevsky observed with venom.

The blood rushed to my face – but Zinaida quickly put her hand on my shoulder, and rising, said in a voice which trembled a little, 'I never gave your Excellency the right to be insolent and, therefore, I must ask you to leave'. She pointed to the door.

'But Princess, I beg you,' muttered Malevsky, turning quite pale.

'The Princess is right,' cried Byelovzorov, and also rose.

'I do assure you, I never imagined . . .,' Malevsky went on. 'Surely there was nothing in my words that . . . I hadn't the remotest intention of insulting you . . . Please forgive me.'

Zinaida looked at him coldly, and coldly smiled. 'Very well, then, stay,' she said, with a careless gesture of the hand. 'There was no reason for me and M'sieu Woldemar to be so angry. You find it amusing to sting . . . I hope you enjoy it.'

'Forgive me,' said Malevsky once again. While I, thinking of Zinaida's gesture, reflected again that no real queen could have shown a presumptuous mortal the door with greater dignity.

The game of forfeits continued for a short time after this little incident. Everyone was slightly embarrassed, not so much on account of the scene itself, but because of another undefined but oppressive feeling. No one mentioned it, yet everyone was conscious of it in himself and in his neighbour. Maidanov read us his verses – and Malevsky praised them with exaggerated warmth.

'How kind he is trying to seem now,' Looshin whispered to me.

We soon dispersed. Zinaida suddenly became pensive. The princess sent word that she had a headache; Nirmatsky began to complain of his rheumatism.

For a long time I could not sleep. I was deeply affected by Zinaida's story. Can there have been some hidden meaning in it? I kept asking myself. At whom, at what, could she have been hinting? And if there really was something to hint at – how could one be sure . . .

'No, no, it cannot be,' I kept whispering, turning from one hot cheek to the other . . . but I would recall the expression on Zinaida's face as she told her story, and I remembered the remark with which Looshin had burst out in the Neskootchny Gardens, the sudden changes in her behaviour to me, and could find no answer. 'Who is he?' These three words seemed to stand before my eyes in the darkness. It was as if a low, malignant cloud were suspended over me – I felt its weight and waited from moment to moment for it to burst. I had become used to a great deal of late, had seen too much at the Zasyekins';

their untidy lives, the greasy candle-ends, the broken knives and forks, the gloomy Vonifaty, the shabby maids, the manners of the old princess herself; this queer form of life no longer surprised me.

But there was something which I now fancied I dimly perceived in Zinaida, something to which I could not reconcile myself . . . An adventuress my mother had once called her. An adventuress – she, my idol, my goddess! The word seared me like a flame, I tried to escape from it into my pillow. I burned with indignation, yet at the same time what would I not have done, what would I not have given, to be that darling of fortune, the man by the fountain!

My blood was on fire and whirling within me. 'The garden – the fountain,' I thought. 'I will go to the garden.' I dressed swiftly and slipped out of the house. The night was dark, the trees scarcely murmured; a soft chill fell from the sky; the scent of herbs came floating across from the kitchen garden.

I went round every walk; the soft sound of my own footsteps increased my nervousness and yet gave me confidence; I would stand still, wait and listen to my heart beating fast and heavily. At last I went up to the fence and leant on a thin post. Suddenly – or was it my fancy? – a woman's figure glimmered past, a few paces away. I peered intently into the darkness – I held my breath . . . What was that? Did I hear steps or was this again the beating of my heart? 'Who is it?' I faltered almost inaudibly. What was that again? A smothered laugh? Or the rustling of leaves? Or a sigh close by my ear? I grew frightened . . . 'Who is it?' I repeated, still more softly.

For an instant the air stirred round me. A streak of fire flashed across the sky – a falling star. 'Zinaida?' I wanted to ask, but the sound died on my lips. All at once everything became profoundly quiet round me, as often happens in the middle of the night . . . Even the grasshoppers ceased chirruping in the trees – only somewhere a window squeaked. I stood still for a time, and then went back to my bed, now grown quite cold. I felt a strange excitement as if I had gone to a rendezvous but had not myself met with anyone, passing close by another's happiness.

17

ON the following day I caught only a brief glimpse of Zinaida. She was going somewhere in a cab with the old princess. On the other hand, I saw Looshin – who barely greeted me – and Malevsky. The young count smiled and began talking to me with great affability. Of all the visitors to the lodge he alone had managed to insinuate himself into our house, and succeeded in making himself very agreeable to my mother. My father did not care for him and treated him with an almost offensive politeness.

'Ah, *Monsieur le page*,' Malevsky began, 'delighted to see you; and what is your lovely queen doing?'

His fresh, handsome face was so repulsive to me at that moment, and he was looking at me with such an expression of disdainful amusement, that I did not reply at all.

'Are you still annoyed?' he went on. 'You really shouldn't be. After all, it wasn't I who called you a page – they're usually to be found with queens. But let me tell you that you are not carrying out your duties at all well.'

'Oh, and why not?'

'Pages ought never to leave their mistresses' side: pages should know everything their mistresses do; indeed they should watch them,' he added, lowering his voice, 'day and night.'

'What do you mean by that?'

'Mean by it? I should have thought I had made myself clear enough. Day – and night. In the daytime it doesn't perhaps matter quite so much: it is light and there are lots of people about. But night – that's when anything may happen. My advice to you is not to sleep at night, but keep watch – watch with all your might: remember the garden – at night – near the fountain – that is where you must watch. You'll thank me for this yet.'

Malevsky laughed and turned his back on me. Probably he attached no great importance to the words he had just spoken to me. He was a notoriously successful practical joker, celebrated for his skill in bamboozling people at fancy dress parties – an art greatly enhanced by the almost unconscious mendacity which permeated his whole being. He only wanted to tease me a little; but every word he uttered ran like poison through my veins – the blood rushed to my head. 'Aha! so that's it!' I said to myself. 'I see! So it wasn't for nothing that I felt drawn into the garden! But no! It shall not be!' I cried loudly, striking myself on the chest with my fist, although I was not quite clear about what it was precisely that was not to be. 'Whether it is Malevsky himself who will appear in the garden (he might well have let it slip out about himself – he was certainly impudent enough), or whether it is someone else (the fence round our garden was very low, and there was no difficulty about getting over it), whoever he is, he'll be sorry when he falls into my hands – I wouldn't advise anybody to cross my path. I shall show the whole world and her, the traitor (I actually used the word "traitor") that I know the meaning of revenge!'

I returned to my room, took out of the writing table an English penknife I had recently purchased, felt the sharp edge, and with a frown of cold and concentrated resolution, thrust it into my pocket as if this kind of thing was nothing new or strange to me. My heart rose angrily within me and turned to stone.

All day I wore a stern scowl, and from time to time, with my lips tightly pressed, I would walk up and down, my hand in my pocket clutching the knife grown warm in my grasp, preparing myself long in advance for something terrible. These new unfamiliar sensations proved so absorbing and even exhilarating, that I scarcely thought about Zinaida herself. I saw constant visions of Aleko, the young gipsy – 'Whither, O handsome youth, lie still'; then 'Bespattered art with blood! ... What has thou done? – Nothing.' With what a cruel smile I kept repeating this 'Nothing' again and again to myself! My father was not at home; but my mother, who had for some time been in a state of almost continuous dull exasperation, noticed my look of doom and said to me at supper:

'Why are you sulking like a mouse in a grain-bin?'

At which I merely gave a condescending smile and thought 'If they only knew!'

It struck eleven; I went up to my room but did not undress; I was waiting for midnight; at last it struck. 'Time!' I muttered through my teeth, and buttoning myself up to the throat, and even rolling up my sleeves, I went into the garden.

I had already selected the exact spot for my vigil: at the end of the garden, at the point where the fence which separated our possessions from the Zasyekins' ran into the common wall, grew a solitary pine tree. Standing under its low thick branches, I could observe, as far as the darkness of the night permitted, all that went on round me: at the foot of the tree ran a path which had always been full of mystery for me. Like a snake it wound its way under the fence, which bore the marks of climbing feet, and led up to a round arbour made of thick acacias. I made my way to the pine tree, leant back against its trunk, and began my watch.

The night was quiet and still, like the night before, but there were fewer clouds in the sky, and the outlines of the bushes – even of the taller flowers – stood out more distinctly. The first moments of waiting filled me with agonizing suspense, and almost with terror. I had resolved to stop at nothing, but I was still trying to decide what to do. Should I thunder forth, 'Where are you going? Stop! Tell all – or die!' Or should I simply strike ... Every sound, every rustle and whisper seemed oddly significant and strange. I was ready, I was all alert. I leant forward ... but half an hour passed, then an hour; my blood grew quieter, colder: the thought began to steal into my brain that it had all been quite pointless, that I was actually making myself a little ridiculous – that it was only a practical joke on Malevsky's part. I left my ambush and wandered round the entire garden. All was quiet: not a sound could be heard anywhere: everything was at peace, even our dog slept curled up by the gate.

I climbed up on to the ruined greenhouse and saw the long open prospect of the fields before me, remembered the meeting with Zinaida, and lost myself in thought.

I started . . . I thought I heard the creak of a door opening, then the faint sound of a snapping twig . . . In two leaps I got down from the ruin . . . I stood frozen to the spot. There was a sound – quite distinct – of footsteps, rapid, light, but cautious, in the garden . . . They were coming towards me . . . 'Here he is . . . here he is at last', raced through my heart. Convulsively I whipped the knife out of my pocket and frantically I forced it open. Queer red spots danced before my eyes, and my hair stood on end in an agony of fury and terror – the footsteps were coming straight towards me. I stooped and crouched forward to meet them – a man appeared – O God, it was my father!

I recognized him at once, although he was completely muffled in a dark cloak, and his hat was pulled down over his face. He tip-toed past without noticing me, although nothing concealed me, shrunk, huddled and crouched so low that I was almost level with the ground. Jealous Othello, ready for murder, was suddenly transformed into a schoolboy . . . I was so terribly startled by my father's unexpected appearance that in the first instant I did not even notice where he had come from and where he had vanished. It took me a moment to get up and to ask myself, 'Why should my father be wandering about at night in the garden,' when all grew silent round me again. In my terror I dropped the knife in the grass – but did not even look for it: I felt dreadfully ashamed.

All at once I was quite sober again; on my way back to our house I did, however, go up to my seat under the elder tree and glance up at the window of Zinaida's bedroom. The small, slightly curved window panes gleamed with a dim blue light under the pale radiance of the night sky. All of a sudden their colour began to change. Beyond them I saw – saw quite distinctly – a whitish blind pulled down cautiously and gently to the window sill, and it stayed down, like that, quite still.

'What is all this?' I said aloud, almost against my will, when I was back again in my room, 'A dream, a chance coincidence, or ...?' the ideas which suddenly entered my head were so new and strange that I did not dare let myself dwell on them.

18

I ROSE in the morning with a headache. The tense excitement of the previous day had gone. I was depressed, frustrated and overcome by a new, quite unfamiliar kind of sadness, as if something in me were dying.

'Why are you looking like a rabbit who's had half his brain removed?' said Looshin when he met me.

At luncheon I kept glancing at both my parents in turn: my father was, as usual, calm: my mother, as always, secretly irritated. I sat there and wondered whether my father would presently say something friendly to me, as he sometimes did ... but he showed no sign even of his normal, cold affection.

Shall I tell Zinaida everything? I reflected. After all, it can't make any difference now – it is all over between us.

I went to see her, but not only told her nothing – I did not even get an opportunity for a talk which I longed for. The old princess's son, a cadet about twelve years old, had arrived from St Petersburg for his holidays. He was immediately handed over to me by Zinaida: 'Here,' she said, 'my dear Volodya,' (she had never called me this before) 'is a friend for you. He is called Volodya too. Please get to like him; he is still a wild, shy little thing, but he has a kind heart. Show him the Neskootchny Gardens, take him for walks, take him under your wing. You will do it, won't you? You will. You, too, are so very kind.' She laid both her hands affectionately on my shoulders – I felt utterly lost; the appearance of this boy turned me into a boy too. I said nothing and glared at the cadet, who in his turn stood staring dumbly at me. Zinaida burst out laughing and pushed us at each other: 'Go on, children, give one another a hug!' We did so.

'I'll take you to the garden, if you like,' I said to the cadet.

'Very kind of you, I am sure,' he replied in a husky cadet voice.

Zinaida laughed again – and I saw then that the colour in her face was lovelier than ever before.

There was an old swing in our garden: I sat the cadet on the edge of the thin plank and swung him gently. He sat very stiffly in his small, brand-new uniform of thick cloth, with a wide gold braid, and held on tightly to the cords.

'Hadn't you better unbutton your collar?' I said.

'No, thanks – we're quite used to it,' he said, and gave a short cough.

He was like his sister – his eyes especially recalled her. Looking after him gave me pleasure – and at the same time I felt a dull pain quietly gnawing at my heart: 'Today I really am only a little boy,' I thought, 'whereas yesterday . . .'

I remembered where I had dropped my knife the night before, and found it. The cadet asked for it, broke off a thick stem of cow-parsley, cut himself a whistle out of it, and started playing. Othello whistled a little, too.

But that same evening, how he cried, this Othello, in Zinaida's arms when, having discovered him in a distant corner of the garden, she asked him why he was so sad. I burst into tears so violently that she was frightened.

'What is the matter with you, what is it, Volodya?' she kept saying, and when I neither replied nor ceased crying, she made an attempt to kiss my wet cheek. But I turned my face from her and whispered through my sobs, 'I know everything; why did you play with me? What need had you of my love?'

'I am guilty before you, Volodya,' said Zinaida. 'Oh, I am terribly guilty,' she said, clasping her hands tightly. 'There is so much in me that is dark, evil, wicked ... but now I am not playing with you – I love you – and you haven't an inkling why and how much I love you ... but anyhow, what is it that you know?'

What could I tell her? She stood before me and gazed at me, and I was hers, utterly hers from head to foot, whenever she looked at me. Only a quarter of an hour later I was running races with the cadet and Zinaida, I was playing tag, and no longer crying; I was laughing, though a tear or two filled my swollen eyelids even as I laughed. Round my neck, instead of a tie, I wore Zinaida's ribbon, and I screamed with joy when I managed to catch her by the waist. She did exactly what she liked with me.

19

I SHOULD find it difficult if someone asked me to give a detailed account of what went on within me during the week which followed my unlucky venture into the garden. It was a queer, feverish period; the most violently conflicting feelings, thoughts, suspicions, hopes, joys, pains, tossed and whirled within me in a kind of mad chaos: I was afraid of looking into myself, if a boy of sixteen can be said to do such a thing; I was afraid to face anything – whatever it might be – consciously. I simply tried to get through the day as fast as I could, from morning till night: but then, at night, I slept ... the lightheartedness of childhood came to my aid.

I didn't want to know whether I was loved, and I didn't want to admit to myself that I was not. I avoided my father – but avoid Zinaida I could not. Her presence seared me like a flame ... but what did I care what kind of fire this was in which I burned and melted, when it was bliss to burn and to melt? I gave myself freely to my sensations as they came, telling myself lies and hiding from my own memories, and closed my eyes to what I sensed was coming. This sick, sweet longing would probably anyhow not have lasted long; but suddenly a thunderbolt blasted it, and flung me on to a new and altogether different path.

One day when I came home to dinner from a longish walk, I learned, to my surprise, that I was to dine alone; my father had gone away, my mother felt unwell and had shut herself in her room, saying she did not want any food. I could see by the faces of the footmen that something very unusual had taken place. I did not dare to question them, but one of the pantry boys, called Philip, who was passionately fond of poetry and a beautiful guitar player, was a particular friend of mine, and to him I turned. From him I discovered that a terrible scene had taken place between my parents. (Every word of it could be heard in the maids' room; much of it was in French, but Masha, the lady's maid, had lived for five years with a seamstress from Paris and understood every word.) Apparently my mother had accused my father of being unfaithful to her and of having relations with the young lady next door; my father had at first defended himself but then flared up and said something brutal – 'something to do with Madam's age' – which had made my mother cry; my mother had also alluded to a loan supposed to have been made to the old princess, and then made disagreeable remarks about her and about her daughter too, whereupon my father began to threaten her.

'And what's done all the mischief,' Philip continued, 'is an anonymous letter, and nobody knows who wrote it; there is no other sort of reason why these things should ever come out into the open.'

'Why, was there really something?' I brought out with difficulty, while my hands and feet grew cold, and deep down in my breast something began to quiver.

Philip gave a knowing wink. 'There was. There's no hiding these things. Not but what your father was as careful as could be – but then there is always something you can't do without; you have to hire a carriage or something like that ... and you can't do it without servants, either.'

I sent Philip away and flung myself on my bed. I did

79

not sob; I did not give myself up to despair; I did not ask myself where and how all this had happened; I did not wonder how it was that I had not guessed it earlier – guessed it long ago. I did not even harbour bitter thoughts about my father ... what I had learned was too much for me to manage. The sudden revelation crushed me; all was ended. In one swoop all my flowers were torn up by the roots and lay about me – scattered, broken, trampled underfoot.

20

NEXT day my mother announced that she was moving back to the town. In the morning my father went into her bedroom and stayed with her for a long time alone. No one heard what he said to her, but afterwards my mother wept no longer; she grew calm, and asked for food, but did not herself appear, nor did she change her plans. I remember that I wandered about the whole day, but did not go into the garden and did not once glance at the lodge.

In the evening, I witnessed an astonishing scene; my father took Count Malevsky by the arm through the drawing-room, into the hall, and in the presence of the footman, said to him coldly, 'Some days ago, Your Excellency was shown the door in a certain house; I do not now wish to enter into any kind of explanation with you, but should Your Excellency ever again be good enough to deign to pay me a visit, I shall throw you out of the window. I do not like your handwriting.'

The count bowed slightly, clenched his teeth, seemed to shrink into himself, and vanished.

Preparations began for our return to town, to the Arbat, where we had a house. My father himself probably did not want to stay in the country any longer, but apparently he had managed to talk my mother into not starting a public scandal. Everything was done quietly, without haste. My mother even sent her compliments to the old princess, expressing regret that she was prevented by ill health from seeing her before she left.

I walked about in a daze, as if I had lost my wits, longing for it all to end as soon as possible. One thought kept running in my head: How could she – a young girl and a princess – have brought herself to do such a thing, when she knew that my father was not free, and she could after all have married, say, Byelovzorov? What did she hope for, was she not frightened of ruining her whole future? Yes, I thought, this is it – this is love; this is passion; this is devotion. And I remembered Looshin's words: 'To sacrifice oneself is the height of bliss – for some people.'

Some time later, I happened to catch sight of a pale patch outlined in one of the windows of the lodge. 'Can this possibly be Zinaida's face?' I thought. Indeed, it was, I could bear it no longer. I could not leave without a final good-bye. I seized a favourable moment and went to the lodge.

In the drawing-room, the old princess greeted me with her usual slovenly disregard.

'Your people seem to be getting off in a terrible hurry. Why is that, my dear sir?' she remarked, thrusting snuff into both nostrils.

I looked at her, and a load was lifted from my heart. The word 'loan', which Philip had let drop, had been torturing me. She suspected nothing, or at least I thought so at the time. Zinaida came in from the next room, in a black dress, pale, with her hair let down. Without a word she took me by the hand and drew me out of the room.

'I heard your voice and came out at once. You find it, then, so easy to desert us, you wicked boy?'

'I have come to say good-bye to you, Princess,' I replied, 'probably for ever. You have heard, perhaps, we are leaving?'

Zinaida looked intently at me. 'Yes, I've heard. Thank you for coming. I had begun to think I would not see you again. You must not think too ill of me. I have sometimes tortured you; but still I am not what you imagine me to be.' She turned away and leaned against the window. 'Really, I am not like that. I know that you have a low view of me.'

'I?'

'Yes, you, you . . .'

'I?' I repeated painfully, and my heart began to quiver, as it always did under the spell of her irresistible, in-expressible fascination. 'I? Believe me, Zinaida Alexan-drovna, that whatever you did, however much you make me suffer, I shall love you and adore you to the end of my days.'

She quickly turned towards me, and opening her arms wide, put them round my head, and gave me a strong, warm kiss. God only knows for whom that long farewell kiss was seeking, but I tasted its sweetness avidly. I knew that it would never come again.

'Good-bye, good-bye,' I kept repeating.

She tore herself from my embrace, and was gone. I

went too. I cannot even begin to convey the feelings with which I left her. I never wish to experience them again, but I should count it a misfortune never to have had them at all.

We moved back to the town. It was a long time before I could shake off the past; long before I could begin to work again. My wound healed slowly, but towards my father I actually bore no ill feeling. On the contrary, he somehow seemed even to have grown in my eyes. Let psychologists explain this contradiction if they can.

One day I was walking in the street and to my indescribable joy, ran into Looshin. I liked him for his straightforward and candid nature; besides he was dear to me because of the memories he awoke in me. I rushed up to him.

'Oho,' said he, and knitted his brow. 'So it is you, young man. Let's have a look at you – still pretty yellow; however, the old nonsense seems to have left your eyes. You look like a man and not a lap-dog. That's good. Well, what are you doing? Working?'

I gave a sigh. I did not want to tell a lie and was ashamed to tell the truth. 'Well, never mind,' Looshin continued, 'don't be discouraged. The main thing is to live a normal life and not to be carried away. Otherwise, what's the use? Wherever the wave may carry you, it will always turn out badly. Better a rock to stand on, so long as it's on one's own feet. Now I, you see I've got a cough ... And Byelovzorov, have you heard?'

'No, what?'

'No trace of him. They say he went off to the Caucasus. A lesson to you, young man; and it all comes from not knowing how to break off in time – to break out of the net. Though you seem to have got away quite unscathed. Now mind you don't get caught again. Good-bye.'

I shan't be caught, I thought . . . I shall never see her again.

But I was destined to see Zinaida once more.

21

MY father used to go riding every day. He had an excellent English mare, a chestnut roan, with a long slender neck and long legs. She was called 'Electric'; no one could ride her except my father; she was a vicious and tireless animal. One day he came in to me; he was in an excellent temper, something which had not happened for a long time. He was dressed for riding, and was wearing spurs. I begged him to take me with him.

'We'd better have a game of leap frog,' said my father. 'You'll never keep up with me on your cob.'

'Oh yes I will, I'll wear spurs too.'

'Well, all right.'

We set off. I was on a black, shaggy, frisky little horse, with strong legs; he did, it is true, have to gallop pretty hard when Electric was in full trot, but still we did not lag behind. I have never seen a horseman to equal my father. He looked so fine on his mount, sitting apparently with such effortless ease that the horse itself – as if conscious of it – seemed to take pride in the rider.

We rode through all the avenues, visited the Maidens' Field, took several fences (I used to be scared of the jumps, but my father despised timidity and I ceased to be afraid). Twice we crossed the Moscow river, and I had begun to think that we were going home, particularly as my father had himself noticed that my horse was getting tired, when suddenly he veered away from me at the Crimean Ford and broke into a gallop along the bank. I followed him. Presently he came up to a tall stack of old logs. Here he stopped, leaped nimbly off Electric, ordered me to dismount, gave me his bridle to hold, and telling me to wait for him there, near the stack, turned into a little side street and disappeared. I began to walk up and down beside the river, leading the horses, and scolding Electric, who kept tossing her head and shaking herself, snorting and neighing, and when I stopped, would start ploughing up the earth with her hooves, or whinnied, and bit my cob in the neck – in a word, behaved in every way like the spoilt thoroughbred she was.

There was no sign of my father. An unpleasant raw dampness came drifting from the river. A thin drizzle began to fall softly, tracing a criss-cross pattern of tiny brown spots on the grey timber. I was thoroughly sick of seeing those wretched logs, as I wandered up and down beside them. I was becoming more and more deeply depressed, and still my father did not return.

A night watchman, who looked like some sort of Finn, grey all over, with an enormous helmet like a kettle and a halbert (what was a night watchman doing, of all places, on the banks of the Moscow river?) loomed up near me, and turning his face, wrinkled like an old woman's, towards me, said:

'What are you doing here with these horses, sir? I'll hold them for you, shall I?'

I did not answer him. He began to beg tobacco from me. In order to get rid of him (moreover, I was consumed with impatience) I took a few steps in the direction in which my father had vanished, walked down to the end of the little street, turned the corner, and stopped. In the street, about forty paces from me, before the open window of a small wooden house, with his back to me, stood my father. He was leaning with his chest over the window sill; inside the house, half concealed by a curtain, sat a woman in a dark dress, talking with my father; it was Zinaida.

I was utterly stunned. This, I admit, I did not expect. My first impulse was to run away. 'My father will look round,' I thought – 'I shall be lost.' But an odd feeling, a feeling stronger than curiosity, stronger even than jealousy, stronger than fear, gripped me. I stood still and looked. I strained my ears to hear. My father seemed to be insisting on something. Zinaida would not consent. Her face is before my eyes now, sad and serious and beautiful, and upon it the imprint – impossible to convey – of grief, devotion, love, and a kind of despair – I can find no other word for it. She spoke in monosyllables, without lifting her eyes, and only smiled, submissively and stubbornly. By this smile alone I recognized my Zinaida, as she once was. My father gave a shrug of his shoulders, and set his hat straight on his head, which with him was always a sign of impatience ... then I could hear the words '*Vous devez vous séparer de cette* ...' Zinaida straightened herself and held out her hand. Then something unbelievable took place before my eyes. My father suddenly lifted his riding-crop, with which he had been flicking the dust off the folds of his coat, and I heard the sound of a sharp blow struck across her arm which was bared to the elbow. It was all I could do to prevent myself from crying out. Zinaida quivered – looked silently at my father – and raising her arm slowly to her lips, kissed the scar which glowed crimson upon it.

My father flung away the crop and bounding quickly up the steps to the porch, broke into the house. Zinaida turned round, stretched out her arms, tossed her head back – and also moved away from the window.

Faint with horror, aghast, almost out of my wits, I turned and ran all the way back down the turning, and almost letting go of Electric, I made my way back to the bank of the river. My thoughts were in a dreadful whirl. I knew that my cold and reserved father was liable to occasional fits of fury, but yet I could not begin to grasp what it was that I had witnessed ... and in the same instant I realized that however long I lived, I should always remember Zinaida's particular movement – her look, her smile at that moment. I realized that this image of her, this new image which had so suddenly arisen before me, would live in my memory for ever. Unseeingly I stared at the river, unconscious of the tears which were streaming from my eyes. They are beating her, I thought, beating, beating ...

'What are you doing? Give me the mare.' I heard my father's voice behind me. Mechanically, I gave him the bridle. He leapt on Electric's back. The horse, chilled to the marrow, reared and bounded about six feet forward. But my father soon had her under control. He plunged his spurs into her sides, and hit her over the neck with his fist.

'Bah! The whip's gone,' he muttered.

I remembered the swish and the blow of his whip a short while before, and shuddered.

'Where have you put it?' I asked my father after a short pause.

He did not answer and galloped on. I overtook him. I was determined to see his face.

'Did you get bored waiting for me?' he muttered, through his teeth.

'A little – but where did you drop your whip?' I asked him again.

He gave me a quick glance. 'I didn't drop it,' he said slowly. 'I threw it away.'

He grew pensive and his head fell, and it was then that I saw for the first – and it may be the last – time how much tenderness and passion his stern features could express. He galloped away again, but this time I was unable to catch up with him; I arrived home about a quarter of an hour after him.

'Yes, this is love,' I again said to myself, as I sat that night at my writing desk, on which exercise books and notebooks had begun to make their appearance. 'This is passion.' And yet how could one fail to feel the most furious resentment, how could one bear to be struck by any hand, however dear – and yet, it seems, one can, if one is in love, and I – I imagined . . .

During the past month, I had suddenly grown much older, and my love, with all its violent excitements and its torments, now seemed even to me so very puny and childish and trivial beside that other unknown something which I could hardly begin to guess at, but which struck terror into me like an unfamiliar, beautiful, but awe-inspiring face whose features one strains in vain to discern in the gathering darkness.

That night I dreamt a strange and frightening dream. I fancied that I entered a low, dark room. My father was standing there, holding a riding-crop in his hand, and stamping with his feet. Zinaida was cowering in the corner, and there was a crimson mark, not upon her arm, but upon her forehead ... and behind them both rose Byelovzorov, covered with blood. His pale lips parted, and he made angry, menacing gestures at my father.

Two months later, I entered the University, and six months after that my father died (as the result of a stroke) in St Petersburg, where he had only just moved with my mother and me. Several days before his death he had received a letter from Moscow which upset him greatly. He went to beg some sort of favour of my mother and, so they told me, actually broke down and wept – he, my father! On the morning of the very day on which he had the stroke, he had begun a letter to me, written in French. 'My son,' he wrote, 'beware of the love of women; beware of that ecstasy – that slow poison.'

My mother, after his death, sent a considerable sum of money to Moscow.

22

THREE or four years passed. I had just left the University, and was not quite sure what I ought to be doing – which door to knock at; and in the meantime wasted my time in complete idleness.

One fine evening, I met Maidanov in the theatre. He had contrived to get married and enter government service, but I found him quite unchanged. He still alternated between the same foolish transports followed by equally sudden fits of depression.

'You know,' he said to me incidentally, 'that Madame Dolsky is here?'

'What Madame Dolsky?'

'Surely you've not forgotten? The former Princess Zasyekin, you remember we were all in love with her. Yes, and you too. You remember, in the country, near the Neskootchny.'

'Is she married to Dolsky?'

'Yes.'

'And she is here, in the theatre?'

'No, in Petersburg. She came here a day or two ago; she is going abroad.'

'What is her husband like?' I asked.

'Oh, a very nice fellow and quite well off. Colleague of mine in Moscow. You understand – after that episode ... you must know all about that' (Maidanov gave a meaning smile) 'it was not easy for her to find herself a suitable *parti*. And it did not end there ... but with her brains nothing is impossible. Do go and see her; she will be very pleased to see you. She is more lovely than ever.'

Maidanov gave me Zinaida's address. She was staying in the Hotel Demuth. Old memories began to stir within me ... I promised myself to pay a visit to my 'flame' on the very next day. But various things turned up. A week passed, and then another, and when I made my way to the Demuth, and asked for Madame Dolsky, I was told that she had died four days before, quite suddenly, in child-birth.

I felt a sudden stab at my heart. The thought that I could have seen her, and did not, and would never see her again – this bitter thought buried itself in me with all the force of an unanswerable reproach.

'She is dead,' I repeated, staring dully at the porter, and making my way noiselessly into the street, wandered off without knowing where I was going. The past suddenly rose and stood before me. So that was to be the final answer to it all. So that was the final goal towards which this young life, all glitter and ardour and excitement, went hurrying along. Those were my thoughts as I conjured up those beloved features, those eyes, those curls – in the narrow box, in the dank underground darkness – here, not far from me who was still living, and perhaps only a few steps from where my father lay.

And as those thoughts poured in upon me, and my imagination was busily at work,

> Tidings of death heard I from lips unfeeling,
> Unmoved, I listened,

ran in my head. O youth! youth! you go your way heedless, uncaring – as if you owned all the treasures of the world; even grief elates you, even sorrow sits well upon your brow. You are self-confident and insolent and you say, 'I alone am alive – behold!' even while your own days fly past and vanish without trace and without number, and everything within you melts away like wax in the sun . . . like snow . . . and perhaps the whole secret of your enchantment lies not, indeed, in your power to do whatever you may will, but in your power to think that there is nothing you will not do: it is this that you scatter to the winds – gifts which you could never have used to any other purpose. Each of us feels most deeply convinced that he has been too prodigal of his gifts – that he has a right to cry 'Oh, what could I not have done, if only I had not wasted my time.'

And here am I . . . what did I hope – what did I expect? What rich promise did the future seem to hold out to me, when with scarcely a sigh – only a bleak sense of utter desolation – I took my leave from the brief phantom, risen for a fleeting instant, of my first love?

What has come of it all – of all that I had hoped for? And now when the shades of evening are beginning to close in upon my life, what have I left that is fresher, dearer to me, than the memories of that brief storm that came and went so swiftly one morning in the spring?

But I do myself an injustice. Even then, in those light-hearted days of youth, I did not close my eyes to the mournful voice which called to me, to the solemn sound which came to me from beyond the grave.

I remember how several days after that on which I had learnt of Zinaida's death, I myself, obeying an irresistible impulse, was present at the death of a poor old woman who lived in the same house with us. Covered with rags, lying on bare boards, with a sack for a pillow, her end was hard and painful. Her whole life was spent in a bitter struggle with daily want, she had had no joy, had never tasted the sweets of happiness – surely she would welcome death with gladness – its deliverance – its peace? Yet so long as her frail body resisted obstinately, her breast rose and fell in agony under the icy hand that was laid upon it, so long as any strength was left within her, the little old woman kept crossing herself, kept whispering 'Lord forgive me my sins . . .' and not until the last spark of con- sciousness had gone, did the look of fear, of the terror of death, vanish from her eyes . . . and I remember that there, by the death-bed of that poor old woman, I grew afraid, afraid for Zinaida, and I wanted to say a prayer for her, for my father – and for myself.

SOME OTHER PEACOCKS